RAMONA AND HER MOTHER

BEVERLY CLEARY is one of America's most popular authors. Born in McMinnville, Oregon, she lived on a farm in Yamhill until she was six and then moved to Portland. After college, she became the children's librarian in Yakima, Washington. In 1940, she married Clarence T. Cleary, and they are the parents of twins, now grown.

Mrs. Cleary's books have earned her many prestigious awards, including the American Library Association's Laura Ingalls Wilder Award, presented in recognition of her lasting contribution to children's literature. Her *Dear Mr. Henshaw* was awarded the 1984 John Newbery Medal, and her *Ramona and Her Father* and *Ramona Quimby, Age 8* have been named Newbery Honor Books. In addition, her books have won more than thirty statewide awards based on the votes of her young readers. Her characters such as Henry Huggins, Ellen Tebbits, Otis Spofford, Beezus and Ramona Quimby, as well as Ribsy, Socks, and Ralph S. Mouse, have delighted children for more than a generation.

BEVERLY CLEARY

RAMONA AND HER MOTHER

Illustrated by Alan Tiegreen

SCHOLASTIC INC.

New York Toronto London Auckland Sydney
Mexico City New Delhi Hong Kong

ISBN 0-439-14801-4

36   7 8 9/0

Printed in the U.S.A.   40

First Scholastic printing, May 2000

CONTENTS

RAMONA AND HER MOTHER

1

A PRESENT FOR WILLA JEAN

"When will they be here?" asked Ramona Quimby, who was supposed to be dusting the living room but instead was twirling around trying to make herself dizzy. She was much too excited to dust.

"In half an hour," cried her mother from the kitchen, where she and Ramona's big sister Beatrice were opening and closing the refrigerator and oven doors, bumping into one another, forgetting where they had laid the pot holders, finding them and losing the measuring spoons.

The Quimbys were about to entertain their neighbors at a New Year's Day brunch to celebrate Mr. Quimby's finding a job at the Shop-Rite Market after being out of work for several months. Ramona liked the word *brunch*, half breakfast and half lunch, and secretly felt the family had cheated because they had eaten their real breakfast earlier. They needed their strength to get ready for the party.

"And Ramona," said Mrs. Quimby as she hastily laid out silverware on the dining-room table, "be nice to Willa Jean, will you? Try to keep her out of everyone's hair."

"Ramona, watch what you're doing!" said Mr. Quimby, who was laying a fire in the fireplace. "You almost knocked over the lamp."

Ramona stopped twirling, staggered from dizziness, and made a face. Willa Jean, the messy

little sister of her friend Howie Kemp was sticky, crumby, into everything, and always had to have her own way.

"And behave yourself," said Mr. Quimby. "Willa Jean is company."

Not my company, thought Ramona, who saw quite enough of Willa Jean when she played at Howie's house. "If Howie can't come to the brunch because he has a cold, why can't Willa Jean stay home with their grandmother, too?" Ramona asked.

"I really don't know," said Ramona's mother. "That isn't the way things worked out. When the Kemps asked if they could bring Willa Jean, I could hardly say no."

I could, thought Ramona, deciding that since Willa Jean, welcome or not, was coming to the brunch, she had better prepare to defend her possessions. She went to her room, where she swept her best crayons and drawing paper into

14

a drawer and covered them with her pajamas. Her Christmas roller skates and favorite toys, battered stuffed animals that she rarely played with but still loved, went into the corner of her closet. There she hid them under her bathrobe and shut the door tight.

But what could she find to amuse Willa Jean? If Willa Jean did not have something to play with, she would run tattling to the grown-ups. "Ramona hid her toys!" Ramona laid a stuffed snake on her bed, then doubted if even Willa Jean could love a stuffed snake.

What Ramona needed was a present for Willa Jean, a present wrapped and tied with a good hard knot, a present that would take a long time to unwrap. Next to receiving presents, Ramona liked to give presents, and if she gave Willa Jean a present today, she would not only have the fun of giving, but of knowing the grown-ups would think, Isn't Ramona kind, isn't she generous to give Willa Jean a present? And so soon after Christmas, too. They would look at Ramona in her new red-and-green-plaid slacks and red turtleneck sweater and say, Ramona is one of Santa's helpers, a regular little Christmas elf.

Ramona smiled at herself in the mirror and was pleased. Two of her most important teeth were only halfway in, which made her look like a jack-o'-lantern, but she did not mind. If she had grown-up teeth, the rest of her face would catch up someday.

Over her shoulder she saw reflected in the mirror a half-empty box of Kleenex on the floor beside her bed. Kleenex! That was the answer to a present for Willa Jean. She ran into the kitchen, where Beezus was beating muffin batter while her father fried sausages and her mother struggled to unmold a large gelatine salad onto a plate covered with lettuce.

"A present is a good idea," agreed Mrs.

16

Quimby when Ramona asked permission, "but a box of Kleenex doesn't seem like much of a present." She shook the mold. The salad refused to slide out. Her face was flushed and she glanced at the clock on the stove.

Ramona was insistent. "Willa Jean would like it. I know she would." There was no time for explaining what Willa Jean was to do with the Kleenex.

Mrs. Quimby was having her problems with the stubborn salad. "All right," she consented. "There's an extra box in the bathroom cupboard." The salad slid slowly from the mold and rested, green and shimmering, on the lettuce.

By the time Ramona had wrapped a large box of Kleenex in leftover Christmas paper, the guests had begun to arrive. First came the Huggins and McCarthys and little Mrs. Swink in a bright-green pants suit. Umbrellas were leaned outside the front door, coats taken into the bedroom, and the usual grown-up remarks exchanged. "Happy New Year!" "Good to see you!" "We thought we would have to swim over, it's raining so hard." "Do you think this rain will ever stop?" "Who says it's raining?" "This is good old Oregon sunshine!" Ramona felt she had heard that joke one million times, and she was only in the second grade.

Then Mr. Huggins said to Ramona's father, "Congratulations! I hear you have a new job."

"That's right," said Mr. Quimby. "Starts tomorrow."

"Great," said Mr. Huggins, and Ramona silently agreed. Having a father without a job had been hard on the whole family.

Then Mrs. Swink smiled at Ramona and said, "My, Juanita, you're getting to be a big girl. How old are you? I can't keep track."

Should Ramona tell Mrs. Swink her name was

not Juanita? No, Mrs. Swink was very old and should be treated with courtesy. Last year Ramona would have spoken up and said, My name is not Juanita, it's Ramona. Not this year. The room fell silent as Ramona answered, "I'm seven and a half right now." She was proud of herself for speaking so politely.

There was soft laughter from the grown-ups, which embarrassed Ramona. Why did they have to laugh? She *was* seven and a half right now. She would not be seven and a half forever.

Then the Grumbies arrived, followed by Howie's mother and father, the Kemps, and of course Willa Jean. Although Willa Jean was perfectly capable of walking, her father was carrying her so she would not get her little white shoes and socks wet. Willa Jean in turn was carrying a big stuffed bear. When Mr. Kemp set his daughter down, her mother peeled off her coat, one arm at a time so Willa Jean would not have to let go of her bear.

There stood usually messy Willa Jean in a pink dress with tiny flowers embroidered on the collar. Her curly blond hair, freshly washed, stood out like a halo. Her blue eyes were the color of the plastic handle on Ramona's toothbrush. When she smiled, she showed her pearly little baby teeth. Willa Jean was not messy at all.

Ramona in her corduroy slacks and turtleneck sweater suddenly felt big and awkward beside her little guest and embarrassed to have jack-o'-lantern teeth.

And the things those grown-ups said to Willa Jean! "Why, hello there, sweetheart!" "My, don't you look like a little angel!" "Bless your little heart. Did Santa bring you the great big bear?" Willa Jean smiled and hugged her bear. Ramona noticed she had lace ruffles sewn to the seat of her underpants.

"What is your bear's name, dear?" asked Mrs. Swink.

"Woger," answered Willa Jean.

Mrs. Kemp smiled as if Willa Jean had said something clever and explained, "She named her bear Roger after the milkman."

Mrs. Quimby said with amusement, "I remember when Ramona named one of her dolls Chevrolet after the car." Everyone laughed.

She didn't have to go and tell that, thought Ramona, feeling that her mother had betrayed her by telling, as if it were funny, something she had done a long time ago. She still thought Chevrolet was a beautiful name, even though she was old enough to know that dolls were not usually named after cars.

"See my bear?" Willa Jean held Woger up for Ramona to admire. Because everyone was watching, Ramona said politely, "He's a nice bear." And he was a nice bear, the nicest bear

Ramona had ever seen. He was big and soft with a kindly look on his furry face and—this was the best part—each of his four big paws had five furry toes. You could count them, five on each paw. Even though Ramona felt she should be outgrowing bears, she longed to hold that bear, to put her arms around him, hug him close and love him. "Would you like me to hold the bear for you?" she asked.

"No," said Willa Jean.

"Ramona," whispered Mrs. Quimby, "take Willa Jean into the kitchen and sit her at the table so she won't spill orange juice on the carpet." Ramona gave her mother a balky look, which was returned with her mother's you-do-it-or-you'll-catch-it look. Mrs. Quimby was not at her best when about to serve a meal to a living room full of guests.

In the kitchen Willa Jean set Woger carefully on the chair before she climbed up beside him, displaying her ruffled underpants, and grasped her orange juice with both hands, dribbling some down the front of her fresh pink dress.

Mrs. Quimby, assisted by Beezus, set out a platter of scrambled eggs and another of bacon and sausage beside the gelatine salad. Hastily she snatched two small plates from the cupboard and dished out two servings of brunch, which she set in front of Ramona and Willa Jean. Beezus, acting like a grown-up, filled a basket with muffins and carried it into the dining room. Guests took plates from the stack at the end of the table and began to serve themselves.

Ramona scowled. If Beezus got to eat in the living room with the grown-ups, why couldn't she? She was no baby. She would not spill.

"Be a good girl!" whispered Mrs. Quimby, who had forgotten the marmalade.

I'm trying, thought Ramona, but her mother was too flurried to notice her efforts. Willa Jean took one bite of scrambled eggs and then went to work, patting the rest flat on her plate with the back of her spoon.

Ramona watched her charge give her egg a final pat with the back of her spoon, pick up her bear, and trot off to the living room, leaving Ramona alone to nibble a muffin, think, and look at her artwork, arithmetic papers, and some cartoons her father had drawn, which had been taped to the refrigerator door for the family to admire. Nobody missed Ramona, all alone out there in the kitchen. Conversation from the living room was boring, all about high prices and who would be the next president, with no mention of children or anything interesting until someone said, "Oops. Careful, Willa Jean."

Then Mrs. Kemp said, "No-no, Willa Jean. Mustn't put your fingers in Mr. Grumbie's marmalade. It's sticky."

Mrs. Quimby slipped into the kitchen to see

if the coffee was ready. "Ramona, it's time to take Willa Jean to your room and give her your present," she whispered.

"I changed my mind," said Ramona.

Mr. Quimby, refilling the muffin basket, overheard. "Do as your mother says," he ordered in a whisper, "so that kid will give us a little peace."

Ramona considered. Should she make a fuss? What would a fuss accomplish? On the other hand, if she gave Willa Jean her present, maybe she would have a chance to hold that lovable bear for a little while.

"OK," Ramona agreed without enthusiasm.

Mrs. Quimby followed Ramona into the living room. "Willa Jean," she said. "Ramona has a present for you. In her room."

Willa Jean's attention was caught.

"Go with Ramona," Mrs. Quimby said firmly.

Willa Jean, still clutching her bear, went.

"Here." Ramona thrust the package at Willa Jean, and when her guest set her bear on the bed, Ramona started to pick him up.

Willa Jean dropped the package. "Woger's my bear," she said, and ran off to the living room with him. In a moment she returned bearless to pull and yank and tear the wrapping from the package. "That's not a present." Willa Jean looked cross. "That's Kleenex."

"But it's your very own," said Ramona. "Sit down and I'll show you what to do." She broke the perforation in the top of the box and pulled out one pink sheet and then another. "See. You can sit here and pull out all you want because it's your very own. You can pull out the whole box if you want." She did not bother telling Willa Jean that she had always wanted to pull out a whole box of Kleenex, one sheet after another.

Willa Jean looked interested. Slowly she

27

pulled out one sheet and then a second. And another and another. She began to pull faster. Soon she was pulling out sheet after sheet and having such a good time that Ramona wanted to join the fun.

"It's mine," said Willa Jean when Ramona reached for a tissue. Willa Jean got to her feet and, pulling and flinging, ran down the hall to the living room. Ramona followed.

"See me!" Willa Jean ordered the grown-ups as she ran around pulling and flinging Kleenex all over the room. Guests grabbed their coffee mugs and held them high for safety.

"No-no, Willa Jean," said Mrs. Kemp. "Mrs. Quimby won't like you wasting her Kleenex."

"It's mine!" Willa Jean was carried away by the joy of wasting Kleenex and being the center of attention at the same time. "Ramona gave it to me."

Ramona looked around for the bear, which

28

was sitting on Mr. Grumbie's lap. "Would you like me to hold Roger?" Ramona asked, careful not to say Woger.

"No." The bear's owner saw through Ramona's scheme. "Woger wants to sit *there*." Mr. Grumbie did not look particularly pleased.

Willa Jean's parents made no effort to stop their daughter's spree of pull and fling. Ramona watched, feeling much older than she had earlier in the day. She also felt awkward while Beezus moved around the living room, dodging Willa Jean and pouring coffee as if she were a grown-up herself.

At first guests were amused by Willa Jean. But amusement faded as coffee mugs had to be rescued every time Willa Jean passed by. Pink Kleenex littered the room. Ramona heard Mr. Huggins whisper, "How much Kleenex in a box anyway?"

Mrs. McCarthy answered, "Two hundred and fifty sheets."

"That's a lot of Kleenex," said Mr. Huggins.

When Willa Jean came to the last piece of Kleenex, she climbed on the couch and carefully laid it on Mr. Grumbie's bald head. "Now you have a hat," she said.

Conversation died, and the party died, too. No one called Willa Jean an angel now or blessed her little heart.

The Grumbies were first to leave. Mr. Grumbie handed the bear to Willa Jean's mother as Willa Jean filled her arms with pink tissues and tossed them into the air. "Whee!" she cried, and scooped up another armful. "Whee!"

Their departure seemed to be a signal for everyone to leave. "Don't you want to take the Kleenex with you?" Mrs. Quimby asked Willa Jean's mother. "We can put it in a bag."

"That's all right. Willa Jean has had her fun."
Mrs. Kemp was helping Willa Jean into her coat.

"By-by," said Willa Jean prettily as her father
carried her and Woger out the door.

Other guests were telling Mr. and Mrs. Quimby how much they had enjoyed the brunch.
Beezus was standing beside them as if it had
been her party, too. Mrs. McCarthy smiled. "I
can see you are your mother's girl," she said.

"I couldn't get along without her," Mrs. Quimby replied generously.

"Good-by, Juanita," said little Mrs. Swink.

"Good-by, Mrs. Swink," answered Ramona,
polite to the end.

She tossed an armful of Kleenex into the air
so that her mother might notice her, too. Somehow tossing someone else's pulled-out Kleenex
was not much fun, and Mrs. Quimby was so
busy saying good-by to other guests she did not
pay attention.

At last the door was closed, and from the porch where the neighbors were opening umbrellas, Ramona's sharp ears caught her name. "Willa Jean certainly reminds me of Ramona when she was Willa Jean's age," someone said.

And someone else answered, "She's Ramona all over again, all right."

Ramona was filled with indignation. Willa Jean is *not* me all over again, she thought fiercely. I was never such a pest.

"Whew!" said Mr. Quimby. "That's over. What's the matter with those people, letting the kid show off like that?"

"Too much grandmother, I suppose," answered Mrs. Quimby. "Or maybe it's easier for them to ignore her behavior."

"Come on, let's all pitch in and clean up this place," said Mr. Quimby. "Ramona, you find a bag and pick up all the Kleenex."

"Kleenex is made of trees," said Beezus, already helping her mother collect coffee mugs from the living room. "We shouldn't waste it." Lately Beezus had become a friend of trees.

"Put the bag of Kleenex in the cupboard in the bathroom," said Mrs. Quimby, "and let's all remember to use it."

I never was as awful as Willa Jean, Ramona told herself as she went to work collecting two hundred and fifty pieces of scattered pink Kleenex. I just know I wasn't. She followed the trail of Kleenex back to her bedroom, and when the two hundred and fiftieth piece was stuffed in the bag, she leaned against her dresser to study herself in the mirror.

How come nobody ever calls me my mother's girl? Ramona thought. How come Mother never says she couldn't get along without me?

2

SLACKS FOR ELLA FUNT

The day Ramona's father went to work at the check-out counter of the Shop-Rite Market, life in the Quimby household changed. Sometimes Mr. Quimby worked all day; sometimes he worked afternoons and evenings. Sometimes he took the car to work while Mrs. Quimby took the bus to her job in Dr. Hobson's office. Sometimes she drove the car while he took the bus, or one would drop the other off at work.

35

Life was different for Ramona, too. She now went home with Howie Kemp after school. The Quimbys paid Howie's grandmother to look after Ramona until one of her parents could come for her after work. Mrs. Quimby said she could not hold a job unless she knew where Ramona was. Every single minute. Beezus also went to the Kemps' house after school unless she telephoned her mother for permission to go to a friend's house. Ramona had no choice.

One rainy Saturday morning, when Mr. Quimby had worked at the market for several weeks, Ramona asked her mother, "Where do you have to go today?" Mr. Quimby always worked Saturday, the busiest day at the market, which meant Mrs. Quimby had the use of the car to run errands. Ramona was concerned about her mother's errands because she always had to go with her, or as she thought of it, be dragged along. Most of them were of no interest to her.

Mrs. Quimby thought a moment before she said in surprise, "Well, what do you know? No place. We have groceries in the cupboard. No one needs to go shopping for shoes. No one needs a present to take to a birthday party. I can stay home."

"Then what are you going to do?" asked Ramona. She hoped her mother would not decide to clean house.

"Sew," answered Mrs. Quimby. "I've been trying to finish a blouse for weeks."

Sewing seemed like a cozy way to spend a rainy morning. Ramona watched her mother get out the portable sewing machine and set it on the dining-room table along with a pattern and bundle of fabric.

"I'm going to wash my hair," announced Beezus.

"Again?" inquired Mrs. Quimby. "You washed it only day before yesterday."

"But it's so oily," complained Beezus.

"Don't worry, it's just your age," reassured Mrs. Quimby. "You'll outgrow it."

"Yes," said Beezus gloomily. "In about a million years when I'm too old to care."

"You'll never be that old," said Mrs. Quimby. "I promise."

Ramona, bored with her sister's daily complaints about oily hair, leaned on the dining-room table to watch her mother.

"I like it when you stay home," she remarked, thinking of the days before her mother had gone to work when the house had smelled of baking cookies or homemade bread on Saturday morning. "Can I sew, too?" she asked, picturing a companionable morning close to her mother. She imagined a neighbor dropping in and saying, Ramona is her mother's girl, as the two of them stitched away together. Yes, her mother would answer, I can't get along without Ramona.

"Of course you may sew. You know where the scrap bag is," answered her mother with a smile. "What would you like to make?"

"I'll have to think," Ramona said. She went to her room and in a moment returned with a tired-looking stuffed elephant and a large piece of red-and-white checked cloth left over from a dress her mother had made for her when she was in kindergarten. Ramona had liked that dress because it matched the red plastic hat the firemen gave her when the kindergarten class visited the fire department.

Mrs. Quimby looked up from the sewing machine. "I haven't seen Ella Funt for a long time," she remarked as Ramona stood the elephant on its four feet on the table.

"I'm going to make her some slacks," said Ramona as she spread out the fabric. "All my other animals have clothes. Except that snake."

Mrs. Quimby considered. "Slacks for an elephant won't be easy. Why not make slacks for Chevrolet?"

"She's too beat up," said Ramona critically.

"If I were you, I would—" began Mrs. Quimby as Ramona studied the checked cloth.

"I can *do* it," interrupted Ramona, who was impatient with instructions. Mrs. Quimby said no more. The sewing machine began to hum. Ramona picked up her mother's pinking shears and began to cut. There was something satisfying about using pinking shears and watching fabric part in such a neat zigzag line. Working quietly at the table with her mother was even more satisfying. Even the grouchy old cat, Picky-picky, sitting on a corner of the dining-room carpet washing his paws, was behaving like a satisfactory pet.

This morning was a time for sharing con-

fidences. "Mother, did I used to be like Willa Jean?" Ramona asked the question that had worried her since the brunch.

Mrs. Quimby answered when she came to the end of her seam. "You were a lively little girl with a lot of imagination. And you still are."

Ramona was reassured by her mother's words. "I would never throw Kleenex all over the living room when someone had a party," she said virtuously.

If only every Saturday could be like this one: no errands to run, and the two of them sewing and talking together. "Are you going to stop working now that Daddy has a job?" Ramona asked as Beezus, her hair wet but combed, came into the dining room with a paper bag in her hand.

Mrs. Quimby looked up from the collar she was pinning to her blouse. "Why, no," she answered as if she were surprised by the question.

"Why not?" demanded Ramona as Beezus pulled some sewing out of the bag.

"Because we got behind on our bills when Daddy was out of work," explained Mrs. Quimby, "and because we have plenty of ways to use money. Beezus will be ready for college in five years, and in a few more years you will be ready, too."

College, to Ramona, was a faraway school for young grown-ups. When they went to college, their mothers worried about them and mailed them boxes of cookies that they called Care Packages. She had learned this from listening to some of the neighbors talk to her mother. Ramona was surprised to learn that she and her sister would be expected to go to such a school someday.

"Besides," continued Mrs. Quimby, "I like my job. The people are interesting, and Dr. Hobson is pleasant to work for."

"I wish Daddy liked his job." Beezus's head was bent over the skirt she was basting together.

Ramona understood what Beezus meant, because she felt sad, too, and her stomach felt tight when her father came home tired and discouraged after a day in the check-out line. People were in a hurry, many were cross because the line was long, and some customers acted as if he were to blame because prices were so high.

"So do I wish he liked his job." There was a hint of sadness in Mrs. Quimby's voice. "But maybe when he has worked at Shop-Rite longer, he will like it better. New jobs take getting used to."

Ramona held up the two pieces of cloth she had cut out for the front and back of the slacks. Both were the same. Until now she had fastened together whatever she was making with Scotch tape or a stapler. Now Ramona felt the time had come for her to advance. Beezus had been using the sewing machine for several years. "Can I sew on the machine?" she asked.

"If you're careful." Mrs. Quimby demonstrated the use of the machine. Even though Ramona had to stand up to stitch, she found

the machine easier to use than she had expected. She followed her mother's instructions carefully and watched the needle move up and down, leaving behind a trail of tiny, even stitches. Ramona was filled with pleasure at the sight. The sewing machine was much more satisfactory than the stapler, which often stuck or ran out of staples. All sorts of uses for the sewing machine began to fly through Ramona's imagination. Maybe she could even sew paper and make a book. Quickly, but still carefully, she finished the seams of Ella Funt's slacks.

"See? I can use the sewing machine, too," Ramona bragged to Beezus.

Beezus did not bother to answer. She was busy pulling on her skirt while Mrs. Quimby stood by to see how it fit.

Ramona picked up her gray-flannel elephant and shoved its hind legs into the legs of the slacks.

Mrs. Quimby pinned the waistband for Beezus and stood back to look at the skirt. "It fits nicely," she said. "You can go ahead and stitch it." Pleased, Beezus went off to the bedroom to admire her work in the mirror.

Ramona tugged and tugged at Ella Funt's slacks, but no matter how hard she tugged she could not make them come up to the elephant's waist, or to what she guessed was the elephant's waist. Ella Funt's bottom was too big, or the slacks were too small. At the same time, the front of the slacks seemed way too big. They bunched under Ella Funt's paunch. Ramona scowled.

Beezus twirled into the living room to make her skirt stand out. Anyone could see she was pleased with what she had accomplished.

Ramona scowled harder, but no one noticed. No one even cared. The sewing machine hummed. Beezus slipped out of her skirt. Ramona heaved a gusty sigh. The sewing machine stopped humming.

"Having problems, Ramona?" inquired Mrs. Quimby.

"These slacks look terrible." Ramona glowered. "They look awful!"

Mrs. Quimby considered Ella Funt and her slacks. "Well," she said after a moment, "maybe you could find something easier to sew. Slacks for an elephant are very hard to make. I'm sure I couldn't do it."

Ramona could not scowl any harder. "I *like* to do hard things."

"I know you do, and I admire you for it," answered Ramona's mother, "but sometimes it's better to start with something easy and work up."

"Why don't you make a skirt?" suggested Beezus. "Ella Funt is a girl elephant."

"I don't want to make a skirt!" Ramona's

48

voice was rising. "I want to make pants!" She looked at her mother and sister, so calm and happy with their sewing. Why couldn't her sewing turn out right the way theirs did? Ramona felt shut out from something she longed to share. Picky-picky stopped washing, gave Ramona a long stare, and slowly and disdainfully left the room.

"Now Ramona," said Mrs. Quimby gently, "I know you are disappointed, but life is full of little disappointments. You'll get over it. Why don't you try something else? A skirt the way Beezus suggested."

"I won't either get over it!" Nobody had to tell Ramona that life was full of disappointments. She already knew. She was disappointed almost every evening because she had to go to bed at eight-thirty and never got to see the end of the eight o'clock movie on television. She had seen many beginnings but no endings. And even though she had outgrown her tricycle, she was still disappointed because she never could find a tricycle license plate with her name printed on it. Didn't the people who made those license plates care about little girls named Ramona? And then there was that time she had gone to the Easter egg hunt in the park with a big paper bag and had found only two little candy eggs, one of which had been stepped on. Nobody had to tell Ramona about disappointment.

The disappointment of Ella Funt's slacks was not one of life's little disappointments to Ramona. It was a big disappointment because she had failed at something she wanted to do and because she no longer felt she was sharing with her mother. Beezus was doing so instead. "I don't want to do something easier!" yelled Ramona, and hurled poor old Ella Funt and her slacks across the room. As the elephant bounced off the wall, a thought flashed through Ramona's mind. Her mother had not actually said she was not like Willa Jean.

Mrs. Quimby spoke sharply. 'That's enough, Ramona. Calm down."

"I won't calm down!" shouted Ramona, bursting into tears. She fled to that haven of anyone in the family who had tears to shed, the bathroom, where she sat on the edge of the tub sniffling miserably. Nothing was fair. Her mother was always saying everyone must be patient with Beezus when she was cross because Beezus had reached a difficult age, but what about Ramona? Her age was difficult, too—not old enough to sit down with her mother and sew something she wanted to sew and too old to go pulling out a whole box of Kleenex and flinging it all over the house like Willa Jean. People should not think being seven and a half years old was easy, because it wasn't.

As Ramona sat on the hard edge of the tub, feeling sorry for herself and trying to sort out her thoughts, she noticed a brand-new red-white-and-blue tube of toothpaste lying beside the washbasin. How smooth and shiny it looked with only one little dent where someone had squeezed it once. That tube was as good as new, and it was the large economy size.

Ramona was suddenly filled with longing. All her life she had wanted to squeeze toothpaste, really squeeze it, not just one little squirt on her toothbrush but a whole tube, a large economy size tube, all at one time just as she had longed to pull out a whole box of Kleenex.

I'll give it one little squeeze, thought Ramona. Just one teeny squeeze to make me feel better. She seized the tube. How fat and smooth it felt in her hand. She unscrewed the cap and laid it on the counter. Then she squeezed that tube the way she had been told she must never squeeze it, right in the middle. White paste shot out faster than she had expected.

That squirt really did make Ramona feel better. She squeezed again. Another satisfying squirt. She felt even better. This was more fun than finger painting or modeling turtles out of clay. Suddenly Ramona no longer cared what anyone thought. She squeezed and squirted, squeezed and squirted. She forgot about Ella Funt's slacks, she forgot about her mother and Beezus, she forgot that no one ever called her her mother's girl. The paste coiled and swirled and mounded in the washbasin. Ramona decorated the mound with toothpaste roses as if it were a toothpaste birthday cake. When the tube was almost empty, she rolled it properly from the bottom and squeezed some more. Tighter and tighter she rolled it until not another speck of toothpaste could be squeezed out.

There, thought Ramona with pleasure and

satisfaction, which unfortunately lasted only a moment. With the rolled-up tube in her hand Ramona stood looking at the white mound. What would her mother say? What could she do with it? Wash it down the drain? It might foam all over the bathroom. Or it might stop up the sink. Then she really would be in trouble.

Of course just at that moment Beezus came down the hall toward the bathroom. Ramona started to slam the door, but Beezus blocked it with her foot.

Ramona tried to hide the toothpaste by standing tall in front of the washbasin. Unfortunately, she was not tall enough.

Beezus looked over her shoulder. "Is that *toothpaste*?" she asked in disbelief.

Ramona scowled because she did not know what else to do.

"Mother!" Beezus had seen the rolled-up squeezed-out tube. "Ramona has wasted a

whole tube of toothpaste!" Now apparently Beezus was not only a friend of trees, she was a friend of toothpaste as well.

"You keep quiet!" ordered Ramona. "I'll pick it up."

"How?" asked Beezus. "How can you pick up toothpaste?"

"With a spoon. I can put it in a plastic bag with a spoon," said Ramona. "We can dip our toothbrushes in the bag."

"Yuck," said Beezus rudely. "Everybody's germs will get mixed up."

"Picky," said Ramona.

"Girls!" Mrs. Quimby came to see what the argument was about. "Ramona, what on earth got into you?" she asked in exasperation when she saw the toothpaste birthday cake.

The whole thing was much too difficult to explain. Really impossible, so Ramona said cockily, like the funny man on television, "The devil made me do it."

"That's not funny, Ramona." Mrs. Quimby meant what she said.

Ramona did not understand. Everyone laughed when the man on television said the devil made him do something. Why wasn't the remark funny when she said it? Because she was seven and a half (right now!). That was why. Grown-ups could get away with anything. It wasn't fair.

"Get a spoon and a jar from the kitchen," directed Mrs. Quimby, "and scoop up the toothpaste." Then she said to Beezus, "She can use it herself, and the rest of us can use a fresh tube."

Somehow Ramona felt sad knowing she was to be excluded from the family tube of toothpaste for a long time. And she wished her mother would not speak about her to Beezus as if she were not in the room.

"Ramona," said her mother, "don't you ever let me catch you squeezing out a whole tube of toothpaste again."

"I won't," promised Ramona, and as she went off to the kitchen for a jar and a spoon she felt unexpectedly cheerful. She had done something she had always wanted to do. *Of course* she would never squeeze out a whole tube of toothpaste again. She had done it once. She did not need to do it again.

3

NOBODY LIKES RAMONA

In February there came a day for Ramona when everything went wrong, one thing after another, like a row of dominoes falling over. Ramona's mother set it off. "By the way, Ramona," said Mrs. Quimby after breakfast as she hastily tossed potatoes, carrots, and stew meat into the Crock-Pot to simmer while the family was away all day. "Please don't run in the hall in your socks. You might slip and fall."

Ramona's father was next. "And Ramona," he said, pulling strings off celery before slicing it and adding it to the stew, "when you wash your hands, don't leave the dirt on the cake of soap."

Then Beezus. "Or wipe it on the towel."

"I haven't had time to get dirty," said Ramona, who had finished her breakfast. "And I have my shoes on."

"We are talking about yesterday," said her father.

Ramona thought yesterday was a long time ago, hardly worth mentioning. "Everybody picks on me," she said.

"Poor kid." Mr. Quimby kissed his wife on the cheek and each daughter on the top of her head. Then he said, singing the first few words, "Hi-ho, hi-ho, it's off to work I go and at least forty-six changes in produce prices to remember."

Ramona knew her father dreaded Wednesdays, the day prices were changed on fruits and vegetables.

"Maybe things will be easier when you are more used to the job," said Mrs. Quimby. After her husband left to catch the bus, she kissed the girls as if she were thinking about something else and handed Ramona her lunch box and Beezus the brown paper bag that held her sandwich. Seventh-graders thought lunch boxes were babyish. "Scoot along," Mrs. Quimby said. "I have to leave early to take the car for brake adjustment, and then I have to take the bus to work."

"I wish Daddy would get used to his job," remarked Beezus as the sisters plodded toward Glenwood School. Clouds hung low, and the wind was cold. For days the sidewalks had been too wet for roller skating.

"Me, too," said Ramona, who wanted her

parents to be happy so their children could be happy, too. "Why doesn't he find another job?"

"Jobs aren't that easy to get," Beezus explained. "Remember how long he was out of work before he found a job at the market."

Ramona did remember. She remembered how discouraged her father had been after a day of job-hunting and how he had disliked standing in line to collect unemployment insurance.

"It might be easier if he had finished college," said Beezus.

"Why didn't he?" asked Ramona.

"Because he and Mother got married," Beezus explained. "And then they had me." Beezus sounded smug, as if being the first born made her more important to her parents than Ramona.

But I'm the baby, thought Ramona. She was glad when school started; maybe her day would improve in school. Ramona liked Mrs. Rudge, her new teacher, who had taken over the second grade when the former teacher left after Christmas to have a baby. She *thought* Mrs. Rudge liked her, as she liked all the children, but she was not sure exactly where she stood with her. The classroom buzzed softly and busily with the sound of children learning about Indians and cursive writing.

When the morning was half over, Ramona finished her work sheet and was busy filling all the double *oo*'s she could find with crossed eyes and frowns:

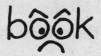

Mrs. Rudge paused beside her desk. Ramona did not have time to hide the frowning *oo*'s.

Mrs. Rudge glanced over Ramona's work

sheet. "Why don't you look again?" she suggested. "Is *like* spelled *l-i-c-k*?"

"I can't spell," said Ramona. "I'm terrible at spelling." That's what her family said whenever Ramona wrote a note. They always laughed and said, "Ramona is no speller. See how she spells *much m-u-c-k*." They behaved as if she had done something clever.

Ramona learned right there that Mrs. Rudge was a teacher who did not accept excuses. "There is no such a word as *can't*," she said, and went on to inspect Becky's work sheet.

How can there be no such word as *can't*? Ramona wondered. Mrs. Rudge had just said *can't*. If there was no such word as *can't*, Mrs. Rudge could not have said there was no such word as *can't*. Therefore, what Mrs. Rudge had said could not be true. Ramona was left with a vague feeling that Mrs. Rudge did not like her because she did not offer to give Ramona extra help in spelling.

At lunchtime when Ramona went into the multipurpose room with her lunch box, she found that she had a leftover-pot-roast sandwich in her lunch. She did not like a leftover-pot-roast sandwich because the meat slid out in big pieces when she bit into it. After chewing awhile she thought, I won't eat it, and she stuffed the rest of her sandwich into the hole in her milk carton and threw it into the trash can. She sat there arguing with herself about how there had to be a word *can't* because she had just thought it. This was not a good day.

After school at the Kemps' house, Ramona and Howie drank the same old apple juice and ate the same old graham crackers that Mrs. Kemp always set out for them. Sticky Willa Jean, holding Woger by one paw, stood and watched. She was wearing a T-shirt with *Grandma Loves Me* printed on the front. The shirt had shrunk so much it showed her navel —tummy button, Mrs. Kemp called it.

Then Howie got out the checkerboard, which he placed on the carpet. Kneeling, he and Ramona began to divide the red and black checkers.

"I want to play." Willa Jean plunked herself down on the carpet, sitting on Woger as if he were a cushion, which was no way to treat a bear, especially a bear like Woger.

"Aw, Willa Jean—" protested Howie, who had his problems with his little sister.

"Now Howie," said Mrs. Kemp, busy with her endless knitting, "play nicely with your sister. She's little, you know."

Howie knew all right.

Willa Jean, pleased to have her grandmother

on her side, set a red checker on top of a black checker. "Your turn," she said to Ramona as if she were being generous.

Ramona and Howie shared one hopeless look.

They were familiar with Willa Jean's original rules for checkers. Ramona set a black checker on top of Willa Jean's red checker. Howie added red and so on in turn until the tower of checkers grew high and crooked. At last, when Willa Jean set a checker on top, the tower tumbled.

"I won!" crowed Willa Jean as Howie tried to prevent scattered checkers from rolling under the couch. "Grandma, I beat Howie and Wamona!"

"Smart girl!" Mrs. Kemp paused in her knitting to smile down upon her granddaughter.

The situation was hopeless. "Let's go down in the basement and see if we can think of something to build," said Howie, and Ramona agreed. They would be undisturbed in the basement. Willa Jean was afraid of the furnace.

Safe from interruption, Howie and Ramona decided to build a boat of the scrap lumber Mr. Kemp collected for Howie to work with.

They had already built a dog, a cat, and a duck decoy that Mr. Kemp said would never fool a real live duck. Now they sawed and pounded until they had a boat with two decks. They were so good at nailing by now they did not even pound their fingers. Next they found a dowel and sawed off two pieces for smokestacks, which Howie studied. "It's going to be hard to nail them to our boat," he said.

"We could use Scotch tape," said Ramona, who felt that almost anything could be accomplished with Scotch tape.

"I don't think it's strong enough for wood," was Howie's objection. "Glue might be better."

"Scotch tape would work if we use lots of it." Ramona was an experienced user of Scotch tape.

In the end, glue won out because Howie thought a boat should look neat. Very, very carefully they spread glue on the ends of the dowels and pressed them in place. They put the top back on the tube of glue, and each held a dowel in place, waiting for the glue to dry. They had not spilled a drop. Fortunately, the glue was quick drying.

"Let's see if our boat will float," said Howie. He pressed the plug of the laundry tub in place and turned on the faucet.

"Howie, what are you two doing down there?" Mrs. Kemp called from the top of the stairs.

"Just seeing if our boat will float," he answered.

"All right," said Mrs. Kemp. "Just don't let the tub overflow."

"We won't," promised Howie.

The boat floated. Howie and Ramona stirred up a storm at sea to make things interesting and watched their boat ride the waves. As it bobbed up and down, Ramona happened to glance up at a shelf above the laundry tub. There she spotted a blue plastic bottle with the picture of a nice old-fashioned lady's face on the label. Bluing!

Ramona knew all about bluing because her mother had used it to make white washing look whiter back in the days before she had gone to work. "If we could get that bottle, we could turn the water blue like a real ocean," she suggested. "It only takes a little bit."

Howie was enthusiastic, but how were they to reach a bottle on such a high shelf? For some reason, Mrs. Rudge's words, there's no such word as *can't*, ran through Ramona's mind. Of course they could get that bottle of bluing.

Ramona managed to balance on her stomach on the edge of the tub. Then she got one knee up and with a boost from Howie was able to climb up onto the edge of the tub. She stood teetering on the narrow edge clinging to the front of the shelf with one hand while she managed to grasp the bottle with the other and

hand it down to Howie. As she did so, the top flew off. Bluing splashed over Howie, who tried to catch the top only to have the bottle slip from his fingers into the tub of water, where it poured forth swirls of beautiful deep blue. Ramona was so startled she lost her balance and landed standing up to her knees in blue water.

"Boy, Ramona, see what you've done." Howie looked down at his shirt and jeans, now streaked with blue.

Ramona felt Howie was being most unfair. She did not spill the bluing on purpose. Besides, why wasn't the top of the bottle screwed on tight? Because some grown-up had not screwed it on, that's why. Children weren't the only people who did things wrong. She fumbled through the blue water, now much bluer than any ocean, and pulled the plug. As the water

74

drained out, she and Howie looked at one another. Now what should they do?

Mrs. Kemp called down the stairway. "It's awfully quiet down there. What are you two up to?"

"We had—sort of an accident," confessed Howie.

Mrs. Kemp came running down the stairs. "Oh, my land!" she cried. "Oh, my goodness!"

Willa Jean began to howl at the top of the stairs.

"Grandma won't let the furnace get you, darling," said Mrs. Kemp. Willa Jean sat down at the top of the stairs and wept.

Mrs. Kemp lifted dripping Ramona out of the tub. Then, right there in front of Howie, she pulled off Ramona's socks, slacks, and blouse and dumped them in the washing machine. Then she pulled off Howie's socks, shirt, and jeans and dumped those in the washing machine, too. Ramona and Howie did not know where to look, they were so embarrassed to be standing there in their underwear. Two years ago they would not have minded, but now that they were in the second grade, they felt that underwear was private.

Mrs. Kemp filled the tub with a few inches of clear water and lifted Ramona back in. Without a word she began to scrub Ramona's feet with a bar of yellow soap. When it was plain that Ramona's feet were going to stay blue, she lifted Ramona out again, pulled a towel out of the dryer, and handed it to her. Then Mrs. Kemp went to work on Howie's blue hands.

When Ramona's blue feet were dry, she asked politely, "What will I wear?" Of course she could not go around in her underwear.

"We'll find something." Mrs. Kemp, rinsing

Ramona's shoes, sounded grim. She held up the shoes, now a strange greenish brown, to let the water drain off them before she leaned them against the furnace to dry.

Suddenly Mrs. Kemp missed Willa Jean. "Oh, my goodness!" she cried, and dashed up the stairs. Ramona and Howie, careful not to look at one another, followed. What Ramona saw made tears come to her eyes. There sat Willa Jean under the dining-room table holding a pair of scissors, sharp scissors, and Woger, who now had only one leg. Willa Jean had cut off Woger's leg! That lovable bear. How could Willa Jean do such a terrible thing? Ramona felt like crying, she loved Woger so.

"Give Grandma the scissors," coaxed Mrs. Kemp. "We don't want the scissors to hurt Willa Jean."

"Boy, Willa Jean." Howie was disgusted.

"What did you have to go and do a dumb thing like that for?"

Willa Jean looked as if her brother had said something unkind. "I wanted to see if Woger had bones," she said.

"He is so soft you should know he doesn't have bones," said Howie. "You didn't have to wreck him."

Willa Jean looked at the stuffing coming out of her bear's wounds and began to cry.

"Never mind, darling," said Mrs. Kemp. "Grandma will sew Woger's leg back on after she finds some clothes for Howie and Ramona."

Ramona was soon bundled into Howie's old shirt and jeans and a pair of ragged sneakers much too big for her. She sat on one end of the couch while Howie sat on the other.

Ramona was cross because she did not like wearing Howie's old clothes. Howie was cross because Ramona had thought of dying the water blue. Both were cross with Willa Jean for spoiling the checker game. Mrs. Kemp, who was sewing Woger's leg back on, was cross with Ramona and Howie, but of course she was not cross with Willa Jean. Only Willa Jean, lying on her back under the coffee table and sucking her thumb, was happy.

This afternoon was not the first time Ramona had been in trouble at the Kemps' house. There was that day she and Howie found Mrs. Kemp's pinking shears. Ramona had been pinking Howie's hair when Mrs. Kemp discovered what they were up to. Ramona had thought she was unreasonably displeased, because Howie's hair was so curly the pinking did not show.

Now Ramona worried. If she got into any more trouble, maybe Mrs. Kemp would not want to look after her. Then her mother could no longer work in Dr. Hobson's office and would have to stay home. Ramona quickly squashed a deep-down thought that she would like to have her mother stay home again. She waited anxiously for Beezus to come. She waited and waited. No Beezus.

Howie looked at a sporting-goods catalog,

turning the pages with blue hands. Boots, quilted jackets with many pockets, and those tents that folded into tiny packages interested Howie. He did not offer to share the catalog with Ramona, even though he knew she liked pictures of duck decoys.

Ramona heaved a gusty sigh. She wished she had brought her Betsy book with her. She enjoyed reading about Betsy because everyone in the book was so nice to her.

When Woger's wounds were mended, Mrs. Kemp started supper. The fragrance of pork chops floated from the kitchen. The younger Mrs. Kemp, Howie's mother, came home with packages and bags of groceries. "Why, hello, Ramona," she said. "I didn't know you were still here."

Mr. Kemp came home from work. "Hello there," he said. "Are you still here?"

Ramona did not know how to answer such a

question. She felt embarrassed, in the way, unwanted. Where was Beezus? What had happened to her parents? Her ears strained for familiar footsteps or the sound of the Quimby car.

"Your mother and father are late today," remarked Howie's mother as she set the table.

Once more Ramona did not know how to answer. Cars were now driving with their lights on. Why didn't someone come? What if her mother and father had been in an accident? Who would take care of Ramona? It seemed as if she might have to sit here on the couch in Howie's old clothes forever.

Ramona began to feel hungry. How good a pork chop would taste! She knew she would not be asked to share the Kemps' supper. With the price of meat these days there would not be an extra chop. Ramona's mouth watered so much she had to swallow. She thought of the pot-roast sandwich she had not finished at lunchtime.

"Ramona, could I fix you some peanut butter and crackers?" asked Howie's mother.

"No, thank you." Ramona pictured a brown chop with mashed potatoes and pool of gravy.

The Kemps sat down at the table with Willa Jean perched on two cushions beside her grandmother, who began to cut her meat for her. And she won't even eat a whole chop, thought Ramona, who felt like a stranger, an intruder in the lives of others. The Kemps said little as they ate. Perhaps they did not want to talk in front of an outsider. Ramona listened to the clink of knives and forks against plates as the Kemps ate their pork chops. She was profoundly embarrassed.

"Willa Jean, darlin', we don't chew with our mouth open," said Willa Jean's grandmother.

At last, when Ramona was blinking back tears because she was sure her parents would never come, the old familiar car turned into the driveway.

"Good-by!" cried Ramona, pulling on her car coat as she ran out the door.

Mr. Quimby was driving, Mrs. Quimby sat next to him, and Beezus was in the back seat. She must have been picked up at a friend's house. "You were late," Ramona informed her family, her voice stern. "You kept me waiting."

"I'm sorry." Mrs. Quimby sounded tired. "It was one of those days. After work when I went to catch a bus to the garage to pick up the car, the bus was late, and when I finally got to the garage, the mechanics hadn't finished the job and I had to wait some more. And I had to keep your father waiting, too."

"What a day!" said Mr. Quimby. "Price changes to remember, and I worked the express line besides." Ramona knew her father disliked the express line in which customers were not supposed to have more than nine items in each basket. Many people tried to slip through with ten or eleven items. Everyone in line was in a hurry and counted the items in one another's baskets. There were arguments. All this un-pleasantness took a lot out of Mr. Quimby.

Please, please like your job, prayed Ramona, forgetting her own troubles for a moment.

Mrs. Quimby turned in the front seat to look at her daughters. Of course she noticed Ramona was wearing Howie's old clothes.

"Ramona, why are you wearing . . . ?" Mrs. Quimby seemed too tired to finish the question.

"Howie and I sort of spilled some stuff and Mrs. Kemp washed our clothes and they aren't dry yet," explained Ramona. Her mother could discover her blue feet later. "It was Willa Jean's fault. She wrecked our checker game so we had to go down in the basement to get away from her."

"Sounds like you," said Beezus. "I can remember when you used to bump the coffee table with your tricycle when I was playing checkers with a friend."

"I did not!" Ramona was indignant.

"You did, too," said Beezus. "You just can't remember."

"Girls!" said Mrs. Quimby. "It doesn't really matter who wrecked whose checker game or where or when."

Rain slanted through the beams of the car lights, the windshield wipers *splip-splopped*, the family was silent. Ramona, huddled in the corner of the back seat, wondered if she really had been as awful as Willa Jean. Nobody loved Ramona—well, maybe her father a little bit sometimes. If her mother really loved her, she would say to Beezus that Ramona was never anything like Willa Jean.

Ramona not only felt unloved, she was so hungry her stomach growled. As Mr. Quimby turned their car into the driveway, she thought of the stew that had been simmering away in the Crock-Pot all day. How good it would smell when they opened the door! The Crock-Pot always gave out a warm and welcoming fragrance as if Ramona's mother had been home all day preparing supper to greet them. One whiff of stew, Ramona was sure, and everything would be all right again. Her mother would forget her troubles with the car, her father would begin to make jokes again, she and Beezus would set the table, and they would all sit down to a nice warm dinner.

4

THE QUARREL

As soon as Ramona stepped through the back door, she knew something was wrong. There was a chill about the house, and it had the faint mustiness of a place that had been closed and unoccupied all day. There was no welcoming fragrance of simmering meat and vegetables. The tiny light on the Crock-Pot was dark, the pot cold.

"Oh, no!" cried Mrs. Quimby, noticing.

"What's wrong?" asked Mr. Quimby, coming in from the hall where he had gone to turn up the thermostat of the furnace.

"Wrong!" Mrs. Quimby lifted the lid of the electric casserole on the kitchen counter. "Someone forgot to plug in the Crock-Pot this morning, that's what's wrong."

The family gathered to peer in at the cold vegetables and raw meat.

"I'm starving!" wailed Beezus.

"Me, too," said Ramona.

"I thought you turned it on," said Mrs. Quimby to her husband as she shoved the plug into the socket. The stew could cook overnight and be warmed up for the next evening.

"Don't look at me," said Mr. Quimby to his wife. "I thought you turned it on." There was an edge to his voice.

For some reason his remark annoyed Mrs. Quimby. "I suppose you think turning on a

91

Crock-Pot is woman's work." The edge in her voice matched the edge in his.

"Not exactly," said Mr. Quimby, "but now that you mention it—"

"Don't forget the time you forgot to fork the potatoes you put in to bake and they exploded," his wife reminded him.

Ramona stifled a laugh at that memory. Her father had looked so surprised the evening the potatoes exploded—*poof!*—when he had opened the oven door.

Mr. Quimby was not going to be drawn into a discussion of past baked potatoes. "Why not just throw the stuff into the frying pan and cook it?" he asked. His idea of cooking was to toss everything into a pan and stir until done. Sometimes he invented interesting dishes with ground meat and eggs, zucchini and cheese. Other times the family tried to be good sports at dinner.

"Because you can't fry stew meat." Mrs.

Quimby sounded annoyed as she looked into the cupboard and the refrigerator. "It's too tough. You know that. Did you bring groceries?"

"No. I thought we were having stew for dinner," answered Mr. Quimby. Crossly, Ramona thought. "I didn't see anything on the grocery list."

Picky-picky, the cat, rubbed against Mrs. Quimby's legs, telling her how hungry he was. "Scat," said Mrs. Quimby.

Picky-picky went to Beezus, not Ramona. He did not like Ramona, had never liked her because she was too noisy.

"I'm practically dying of hunger," said Beezus as she picked up the old cat and rubbed her cheek against him.

"Me, too," said Ramona.

"You girls are no help," Mrs. Quimby told her daughters. "We have a couple of eggs, not enough for an omelet, two strips of bacon, three carrots, and some tired old lettuce. That's it." She looked at her husband. "We don't have to let the cupboard get completely bare before we buy groceries."

This remark gave Ramona a cue. "Old Mother Hubbard went to the cupboard—" she began, but she did not finish the rhyme because she could see no one was listening.

"Anytime we are low on groceries, just make a list," said Mr. Quimby. "That's all you have to do."

"I could make carrot salad," suggested Beezus, as if carrot salad might smooth things over.

"We could have pancakes," said Mr. Quimby, "with half a strip of bacon apiece."

"Not a very nutritious meal," said Mrs. Quimby, "but better than starvation." She reached for a mixing bowl while Beezus, who had dropped Picky-picky and washed her hands, began to grate carrots onto a sheet of waxed paper. Ramona leaned against the counter to watch. She wanted to make sure her sister did not grate her fingers into the salad.

"Ramona, don't just stand there," said Mr. Quimby as he laid the bacon in a frying pan. "Get busy and set the table. As my grandmother used to say, 'Every kettle must rest on its own bottom,' so do your part."

Ramona made a face as she reached for the place mats. "Daddy, I bet your grandmother didn't really say all the things you say she said."

"If she did, she must have been a dreadful bore," said Mrs. Quimby, who was beating batter as if she were angry with it.

Mr. Quimby looked hurt. "You didn't know my grandmother."

"If she went around spouting wisdom all the time, I can't say I'm sorry." Mrs. Quimby was

95

on her knees, dragging the griddle from behind the pots and pans in the bottom of the cupboard.

Ramona paused in laying the silverware to make sure there was no blood on the carrots. She felt the muscles of her stomach tighten as they always tightened when her mother was cross with her father.

"My grandmother was a wonderful woman," said Mr. Quimby. "She had a hard life out there in the country, but she was good to us kids and we learned a lot from her."

"Well, my grandmother wasn't so bad herself." With an angry sounding crash the griddle knocked over two pans and a double boiler as Mrs. Quimby yanked it from the cupboard. "And I learned a lot from her."

Ramona and Beezus exchanged an anxious look.

"Just what did you learn from your grandmother?" asked Mr. Quimby. "As far as I could see, all she ever did was gad around and play bridge."

Ramona and Beezus exchanged another look. Were their parents quarreling? Really quarreling? Yes, the sisters' eyes agreed. Both girls were worried.

Mrs. Quimby set the griddle on the stove with more noise than necessary. She was plainly trying to think what she had learned from her grandmother. Finally she said, "My grandmother taught me to pick flowers with long stems and to pick a few leaves to put in with them."

"Very useful," said Mr. Quimby.

The hint of sarcasm in his voice must have annoyed Mrs. Quimby because she said, "My grandmother didn't have much money, but she had a sense of beauty." The drop of water she flicked on the griddle refused to dance.

"No matter how much my grandmother had

to scrimp and pinch to make ends meet," said Mr. Quimby, "she always managed to find money to buy paper for me to draw on."

Scrimp and pinch to make ends meet, thought Ramona, liking the sound of the words. She would remember them. The smell of bacon sizzling made her feel better. It also made her hungrier.

"My grandmother taught me useful things, too." Mrs. Quimby had had time to think. "She taught me that a dab of spit would stop a run in a stocking." She flicked another drop of water on the griddle. This one danced. The griddle was hot.

"Some grandmother," said Mr. Quimby, "spitting on her stockings."

"You're both being silly," Beezus burst out. "Just plain silly!"

"Young lady, you keep out of this," ordered Mr. Quimby.

Beezus glared at her father. "Well, you are," she muttered.

Mrs. Quimby silently poured four puddles of batter on the griddle. Ramona prayed that the quarrel, whatever it was about, was over.

Beezus stirred mayonnaise into the blood-free carrots, which she then divided on four limp lettuce leaves on four salad plates. Mr. Quimby turned the bacon. Mrs. Quimby flipped the pancakes. Ramona's stomach relaxed. In a moment her mother would slide the pancakes onto a platter and start another four cooking. Ramona could hardly wait, she was so hungry.

"Are you sure those pancakes are done?" asked Mr. Quimby as his wife slid the pancake turner under them. "They don't look done to me."

"They bubbled in the middle before I turned them," said Mrs. Quimby, "and they look done to me."

99

Mr. Quimby took the pancake turner from his wife. Using it as a weapon, he slashed each pancake in the center. Ramona and Beezus exchanged a shocked look. Their father had slashed their mother's pancakes! He had gone too far. Frightened, they watched raw batter ooze from four gashes in the pancakes. Their father was right. The cakes were not done. Now what would their mother do?

Mrs. Quimby was furious. She snatched back the pancake turner, scooped up the oozing cakes, and tossed them into the garbage.

"You didn't need to do that." Mr. Quimby looked amused. He had won. "You could have turned them again and let them finish cooking."

"And I suppose your grandmother made absolutely perfect pancakes," said Mrs. Quimby in a voice stiff with anger.

Mr. Quimby looked calm and even more amused. "As a matter of fact, she did," he said.

"Brown and lacy, cooked all the way through, and with crisp edges."

"The best pancakes you ever ate," stated Mrs. Quimby in a voice that made Ramona silently pray. Mother, be nice again. Please, please be nice again.

"Right," said Mr. Quimby. "Light enough to melt in your mouth."

Be quiet, Daddy, prayed Ramona. You'll make things worse.

"Oh—you!" Mrs. Quimby gave Mr. Quimby a swat on the seat of his pants with the pancake turner before she threw it on the counter. "Bake them yourself since you learned so much from that noble grandmother of yours!"

Ramona and Beezus stood frozen with shock. Their mother had hit their father with a pancake turner. Ramona wanted to fly at her mother, to strike her and cry out, You hit my daddy! She dared not.

Mr. Quimby tucked a dish towel in his belt for an apron and calmly ladled batter onto the griddle while his wife stalked into the living room and sat down with the newspaper. If only he wouldn't whistle so cheerfully as he deftly turned the cakes and drained the bacon.

"Dinner is served," Mr. Quimby announced as he set a platter of hot cakes and bacon on the table and pulled the dish towel from his belt. Silently Mrs. Quimby joined the family.

Even though her mother was usually a much better cook than her father, Ramona had to admit her father made excellent pancakes. Unfortunately, she was no longer very hungry. She felt all churned up inside, as if she didn't know whether to cry or to burst out of the house shouting, My mother and father had a fight!

"Please pass the butter." Mrs. Quimby might have been speaking to a stranger.

103

"May I please have the syrup?" Mr. Quimby asked politely.

"The funniest thing happened at school," said Beezus, and Ramona understood that her sister was anxious to start a conversation that would smooth things over and make their parents forget their quarrel, perhaps make them laugh.

After a moment of silence Mrs. Quimby said, "Tell me."

"You'll never guess how a boy spelled *relief* in a spelling test," said Beezus.

"How?" asked Ramona to help the conversation along. Mr. Quimby silently served himself two more hot cakes.

"He spelled it *r-o-l-a-i-d-s*," said Beezus, looking anxiously at her parents, who actually smiled.

Ramona did not smile. "But the man on television spells *relief* that way. He said *r-o-l-a-i-d-s* spells *relief*. I've heard him."

"Silly," said Beezus, but this time she spoke with affection. "That's just a slogan. *Relief* is *r-e-l-i-e-f*."

"Oh." Ramona was glad to know. Tabletalk sank back into silence while Ramona thought about spelling. Spelling was full of traps—blends and silent letters and letters that sounded one way in one word and a different way in another —and having a man stand there on television fooling children was no help. She was glad she had a big sister who understood those things.

The evening was quiet. Mr. Quimby dozed in front of the television set. Mrs. Quimby took a shower and went to bed to read. Beezus did her homework in her room. Ramona tried to draw a monster eating a mouthful of people, but she could not make the picture on paper match the one in her imagination. Her monster looked as if he were eating paper dolls instead of real people. The house was unnaturally quiet.

The television droned on. Both girls went to bed without being told.

Unhappy thoughts kept Ramona awake. What if her mother and father did not love one another anymore? What if they decided to get a divorce like her friend Davy's parents? What would happen to her? Who would take care of her? Beezus was closer to being a grown-up, but what about Ramona? She wanted to cry but could not. She felt too tight inside to cry. Tears teetered on her eyelashes but would not give her the relief of falling.

Finally Ramona could stand her fear and loneliness no longer. She slipped out of bed and tiptoed into her sister's room.

"Ramona?" Beezus too was awake.

"I can't go to sleep," whispered Ramona.

"Neither can I," said Beezus. "Come on, get in bed with me."

This invitation was what Ramona had been hoping for. Gratefully she slipped beneath the covers and snuggled against her sister. "Do you think they'll get a divorce?" she whispered. "They won't talk to each other."

"Of couse not," said Beezus. "At least I don't think so."

"Who would take care of me if they did?" Ramona felt she had to have the answer from someone. "I'm still little." Beezus, of course, was her mother's girl, but what about Ramona?

Beezus seemed to be considering the question. "I'll try," she said at last.

"You aren't grown up enough," said Ramona, nevertheless comforted. Beezus cared.

"I know," admitted Beezus. "I read a book about a girl who took care of her brothers and sisters when their father died, but that was off in the mountains someplace where they all

picked herbs and things. It wouldn't work in the city."

"Mother and Daddy won't be dead." Ramona was consoled by this knowledge.

Beezus was silent awhile. "They could have been joking," she said. "Sort of."

"But Mother hit Daddy," Ramona pointed out. "On the seat of his pants with a pancake turner."

"I don't think that's the same as if she had hit him with something hard," said Beezus. "After all, she didn't really hurt him."

Ramona tried to find a bright side. "And he didn't hit her back," she said. "But if they loved us, they wouldn't fight." She silently said her prayers, ending with, "Please, please don't let Mother and Daddy fight."

From the kitchen came a whiff of the stew that would simmer through the night for their supper the next evening. Soothed by the homey fragrance, the sisters fell asleep.

In the morning, a few seconds after she awoke and found herself in her sister's bed, a dull, unhappy feeling settled over Ramona. Her parents had quarreled. She dreaded facing them at breakfast. She did not know what to say to them. Beezus looked unhappy, too. Getting dressed took longer than usual, and when they finally went into the kitchen, they were surprised to see their parents sharing the morning paper as they ate breakfast together.

"Good morning, girls," said Mr. Quimby with his usual cheerfulness.

"There is oatmeal on the stove." Mrs. Quimby smiled fondly at her daughters. "Did you sleep well?"

Beezus was suddenly angry. "No, we didn't!"

"No, we didn't," echoed Ramona, encouraged

by her sister's anger. How could her mother expect them to sleep well when they were so worried?

Startled, both parents laid down the newspaper.

"And it's all your fault," Beezus informed them.

"What on earth are you talking about?" asked Mrs. Quimby.

Beezus was near tears. "Your big fight, that's what."

Ramona blinked back tears, too. "You wouldn't even talk to each other. And you hit Daddy!"

"Of course we were speaking," said Mrs. Quimby. "Where did you get the idea we weren't? We were just tired is all. We had one of those days when everything seemed to go wrong."

So did I, thought Ramona.

"I went to bed and read," continued Mrs. Quimby, "and your father watched television. That was all there was to it."

Ramona felt almost limp with relief. At the same time she was angry with her parents for causing so much worry. "Grown-ups aren't supposed to fight," she informed them.

"Oh, for heaven's sake," said Mrs. Quimby. "Why not?"

Ramona was stern. "Grown-ups are supposed to be perfect."

Both her parents laughed. "Well, they are," Ramona insisted, annoyed by their laughter.

"Name one perfect grown-up," challenged Mr. Quimby. "You can't do it."

"Haven't you noticed grown-ups aren't perfect?" asked Mrs. Quimby. "Especially when they're tired."

"Then how come you expect us kids to be so perfect all the time?" demanded Ramona.

"Good question," said Mr. Quimby. "I'll have to think of an answer."

"We want you to be perfect so you won't grow up to bicker about your grandmothers and their pancakes," said Mrs. Quimby. Both parents thought her reply was funny.

Ramona felt the way Picky-picky looked when someone rumpled his fur. Maybe grown-ups weren't perfect, but they should be, her parents most of all. They should be cheerful, patient, loving, never sick and never tired. And fun, too.

"You kids fight," said Mr. Quimby. "Why shouldn't we?"

"It isn't dignified," said Beezus, giving Ramona another word to add to her list. "Especially when you hit someone with a pancake turner."

"Oh, you silly little girls," said Mrs. Quimby with amusement and affection.

"Why should we let you kids have all the fun?" asked Mr. Quimby.

"We don't quarrel for fun," Ramona informed her father.

"You could fool me," said Mr. Quimby.

Ramona refused to smile. "Don't you ever do it again," she ordered her parents in her sternest voice.

"Yes, ma'am," answered Mrs. Quimby with mock meekness, as if she were poking a little fun at Ramona.

"Yes, *ma'am!*" said her father, and saluted as if she were somebody important.

This time Ramona had to laugh.

5

THE GREAT HAIR ARGUMENT

"Ramona, stand on both feet and hold still," said Mrs. Quimby one Saturday morning. "I can't cut your bangs straight when you wiggle."

"I'm trying," said Ramona. Bits of falling hair made her nose tickle. She blew upward, fanning out her bangs from her forehead, to rid herself of the tickle.

"Now see what you've done." Mrs. Quimby recombed the bangs.

Ramona stood perfectly still in an agony of itching, twitching her nose to get rid of snips of falling hair, until her mother finally said, "There, little rabbit, we're finished." She removed the

towel from Ramona's shoulders and shook it over the kitchen wastebasket. Ramona, who liked being called a little rabbit, continued to twitch her nose and think of the warm and cozy picture books about bears and rabbits her mother used to read to her at bedtime before she kissed her good-night. She had loved those books. They made her feel safe. During the daytime she had preferred books about steam shovels, the noisier the better, but at night— bears, nice bears, and bunnies.

"Next!" Mrs. Quimby called out to Beezus, who had just washed her hair. These days Beezus spent a lot of time locked in the bathroom with a bottle of shampoo.

"Beezus, don't keep me waiting," said Mrs. Quimby. "I have a lot to do this morning." The washing machine had broken down, and because no one had been able to stay home during the week to admit a repairman, Mrs. Quimby had to drive to a laundromat with three loads of washing. Repairmen did not work on Saturdays.

"I'm waiting," repeated Mrs. Quimby.

Beezus, rubbing her hair with a towel, appeared in the doorway. "Mother, I don't want you to cut my hair," she announced.

Ramona, about to leave the kitchen, decided to stay. She sensed an interesting argument.

"But Beezus, you're so shaggy," protested Mrs. Quimby. "You look untidy."

"I don't want to look tidy," said Beezus. "I want to look nice."

"You look nice when you're neat." Mrs. Quimby's voice told Ramona her mother's patience was stretched thin. "And don't forget, how you look is not as important as how you behave."

"Mother, you're so old-fashioned," said Beezus.

Mrs. Quimby looked both annoyed and amused. "That's news to me."

Beezus plainly resented her mother's amusement. "Well you *are*."

"All right. I'm old-fashioned," said Mrs. Quimby in a way that told Ramona she did not mean what she was saying. "But what are we going to do about your shaggy hair?"

"I am not a sheep dog," said Beezus. "You make me sound like one."

Mrs. Quimby chose silence while Ramona, fascinated, waited to see what would happen next. Deep down she was pleased, and guilty because she was pleased, that her mother was annoyed with Beezus. At the same time, their disagreement worried her. She wanted her family to be happy.

"I want to get my hair cut in a beauty shop," said Beezus. "Like all the other girls."

119

"Why Beezus, you know we can't afford a luxury like that," said Mrs. Quimby. "Your hair is sensible and easy to care for."

"I'm practically the only girl in my whole class who gets a home haircut," persisted Beezus, ignoring her mother's little speech.

"Now you're exaggerating." Mrs. Quimby looked tired.

Ramona did not like to see her mother look tired so she tried to help. "Karen in my room at school says her mother cuts her hair and her sister's too, and her sister is in your class."

Beezus turned on her sister. "You keep out of this!"

"Let's not get all worked up," said Mrs. Quimby.

"I'm not worked up," said Beezus. "I just don't want to have a home haircut, and I'm not going to have one."

"Be sensible," said Mrs. Quimby.

Beezus scowled. "I've been good old sensible Beezus all my life, and I'm tired of being sensible." She underlined this announcement by adding, "Ramona can get away with anything, but not me. No. I always have to be good old sensible Beezus."

"That's not so." Ramona was indignant. "I never get away with anything."

After a thoughtful moment, Mrs. Quimby spoke. "So am I tired of being sensible all the time."

Both sisters were surprised, Ramona most of all. Mothers were supposed to be sensible. That was what mothers were for.

Mrs. Quimby continued. "Once in a while I would like to do something that isn't sensible."

"Like what?" asked Beezus.

"Oh—I don't know." Mrs. Quimby looked at the breakfast dishes in the sink and at the rain spattering against the windows. "Sit on a cushion in the sunshine, I guess, and blow the fluff off dandelions."

Beezus looked as if she did not quite believe her mother. "Weeds don't bloom this time of year," she pointed out.

Ramona felt suddenly close to her mother and a little shy. "I would like to sit on a cushion and blow dandelion fluff with you," she confided, thinking what fun it would be, just the two of them, sitting in warm sunshine, blowing on the yellow blossoms, sending dandelion down dancing off into the sunlight. She leaned against her mother, who put her arm around her and gave her a little hug. Ramona twitched her nose with pleasure.

"But Mother," said Beezus, "you always said we shouldn't blow on dandelions because we would scatter seeds and they would get started in the lawn and are hard to dig out."

122

"I know," admitted Mrs. Quimby, her moment of fantasy at an end. "Very sensible of me."

Beezus was silenced for the time being.

"I like your hair, Mother," said Ramona, and she did. Her mother's short hair was straight, parted on one side and usually tucked behind her left ear. It always smelled good and looked, Ramona felt, the way a mother's hair should look, at least the way her mother's hair should look. "I think your hair looks nice," she said, "and I don't mind when you cut my hair." In the interest of truth she added, "Except when my nose tickles."

Beezus flared up once more. "Well, goody-goody for you, you little twerp," she said, and flounced out of the kitchen. In a moment the door of her room slammed.

Ramona's feelings were hurt. "I'm not a little

twerp, am I?" she asked, wondering if her mother agreed.

Mrs. Quimby reached for the broom to sweep bits of hair from the kitchen floor. "Of course not," she said. "I don't bring up my daughters to be twerps."

Ramona twitched her nose like a rabbit.

Afterward neither Mrs. Quimby nor Beezus mentioned hair. Beezus's hair grew shaggier and Ramona decided that if her sister did not look like a sheep dog yet, she soon would. She also sensed that, as much as her mother wanted to say something about Beezus's hair, she was determined not to.

Beezus, on the other hand, looked defiant. She sat at the dinner table with a you-can't-make-me-if-I-don't-want-to look on her face.

Ramona discovered that the tiny part of her-

125

self, deep down inside, that had been pleased because her mother was angry with her sister was no longer pleased. Anger over one person's hair was not worth upsetting the family.

"Women," muttered Mr. Quimby every evening at supper. He also remarked, as if he had hair on his mind, that he thought he was getting a little thin on top and maybe he should massage his scalp.

Conversation was strained. Beezus avoided speaking to her mother. Mrs. Quimby tried to look as if nothing had happened. She said calmly, "Beezus, when the shampoo bottle is almost empty, don't forget to add shampoo to the grocery list. We use it, too, you know."

"Yes, Mother," said Beezus.

Ramona felt like yelling, Stop it, both of you! She tried to think of interesting things to talk about at the dinner table to make her family forget about hair.

One evening, to distract her family from hair, Ramona was telling how her teacher had explained that the class should not be afraid of big words because big words were often made up of little words: *dishcloth* meant a cloth for washing dishes and *pancake* meant a cake cooked in a pan.

"But I bake cakes in pans—or used to—and this does not make them pancakes," Mrs. Quimby pointed out. "If I bake an angelfood cake in a pan, it is not a pancake."

"I know," said Ramona. "I don't understand it because *carpet* does not mean a pet that rides in a car. Picky-picky is not a carpet when we take him to the vet." At this example her parents laughed, which pleased Ramona until she noticed that Beezus was neither laughing nor listening.

Beezus took a deep breath. "Mother," she said in a determined way that told Ramona her sister was about to say something her mother might not like. The words came out in a rush. "Some of the girls at school get their hair cut at Robert's School of Hair Design. People who are learning to cut hair do the work, but a teacher watches to see that they do it right. It doesn't cost as much as a regular beauty shop. I've saved my allowance, and there's this lady named Dawna who is really good and can cut hair so it looks like that girl who ice skates on TV. You know, the one with the hair that sort of floats when she twirls around and then falls in place when she stops. Please, Mother, I have enough money saved." When Beezus had finished this speech she sat back in her chair with an anxious, pleading expression on her face.

Mrs. Quimby, who had looked tense when Beezus first began to speak, relaxed. "That seems reasonable. Where is Robert's School of Hair Design?"

"In that new shopping center on the other side of town," Beezus explained. "Please, Mother, I'll do anything you want if you'll let me go."

Ramona did not take this promise seriously.

In the interests of family peace, Mrs. Quimby relented. "All right," she said with a small sigh. "But I'll have to drive you over. If you can hold out until Saturday, we'll go see what Dawna can do about your hair after I drive your father to work."

"Oh, thank you, Mother!" Beezus looked happier than she had since the beginning of the great hair argument.

Ramona was pleased, too, even though she knew she would have to be dragged along. Peace in the family was worth a boring morning.

Saturday turned out to be cold, raw, and wet. Ramona despaired of ever using her roller skates. The Quimbys hurried through breakfast, stacked the dishes in the sink, piled into the car and drove off, windshield wipers flopping furiously, to deliver Mr. Quimby to the Shop-Rite Market. Ramona, resigned to a tiresome morning, could feel Beezus's excitement and see how tightly she clutched her allowance in the drawstring bag she had crocheted.

When Mr. Quimby had been dropped off at the market, Beezus joined her mother in the front seat. She always gets to sit in the front seat, thought Ramona.

Mrs. Quimby started up the on-ramp to the freeway that cut the city in two. "Beezus, watch for the signs. I have to keep my eyes on my driving," she directed.

Ramona thought, I can read, too, if the words aren't too long.

Mrs. Quimby looked back over her shoulder for a space in which to merge with the heavy morning traffic. A space came down the free-way, and Mrs. Quimby managed to fit the car into it. In no time they were crossing the river, which looked cold and gray between the black girders of the bridge. Green signs spanned the freeway.

"Do I turn left?" asked Mrs. Quimby, uncertain of the way to the shopping center.

"Right," said Beezus.

Mrs. Quimby turned right onto the off-ramp.

"Mother," cried Beezus. "You were supposed to turn left."

"Then why did you tell me to turn right?" Mrs. Quimby sounded angry.

"You asked if you should turn left," said Beezus, "and I meant, 'Right, you should turn left'."

"After this, use your head," said Mrs. Quimby. "Now how do I get back on the freeway?" She drove through a maze of unfamiliar one-way streets looking for an on-ramp sign. Finally she asked for directions from a man at a service station. He looked disagreeable because he had to come out in the rain.

Ramona sighed. The whole world seemed gray and cross, and it was most unfair that she should have to be dragged along on a dreary ride just because Beezus wanted her hair cut by

Dawna. Her mother would never go to all this trouble for Ramona's hair. Huddled in the back seat, she began to feel carsick. The Quimby car, which they had bought from someone who had owned a large dog, began to smell like a dog. "Oh-h," moaned Ramona, feeling sick. She thought about the oatmeal she had eaten for breakfast and quickly tried not to think about it.

Mrs. Quimby glanced in the rear-view mirror. "Are you all right, Ramona?" Her voice was anxious.

Ramona did not answer. She was afraid to open her mouth.

"I think she's going to upchuck," said Beezus, who, since she was in the seventh grade, said *upchuck* instead of *throw up*. She felt the new word was more sophisticated.

"Hang on, Ramona!" said Mrs. Quimby. "I can't stop on the freeway, and there's no way to get off."

"Mother!" cried Beezus. "She's turning green!"

"Ramona, open the window and hang on!" ordered Mrs. Quimby.

Ramona was too miserable to move. Beezus understood. She unbuckled her seat belt, which

buzzed angrily. "Oh, shut up," she said to her seat belt as she leaned over and lowered a window for Ramona.

Cold air swept away the doggy smell, and drops of rain against her face made Ramona feel better, but she kept her mouth shut and did not move. Hanging on was not easy.

"How did I ever get into this?" Mrs. Quimby wondered aloud as she turned onto the off-ramp that led from the freeway.

When the haircut expedition finally reached the shopping center and parked near Robert's School of Hair Design, the three Quimbys splashed through the rain. Ramona, who had quickly recovered when the car stopped, found a certain grim pleasure in stomping in puddles with her boots.

After the cold, the air inside the beauty school seemed too warm and too fragrant. Pee-you, thought Ramona as she listened to running water, snipping scissors, and the hushed roar of hair dryers.

A man, probably Robert himself, asked, "What can I do to help you ladies?" as perspiring Ramona began to wiggle out of her car coat.

Beezus was suddenly shy. "I—I would like Dawna to cut my hair," she said in almost a whisper.

"Dawna graduated last week," said Robert, glancing behind the screen that hid the activity of the school, "but Lester can take you."

"Go ahead," said Mrs. Quimby, answering Beezus's questioning eyes. "You want your hair cut."

When Robert asked for payment in advance, Beezus pulled open her crocheted bag and unfolded the bills she had saved. As Robert led her behind the screen, Mrs. Quimby sank with a little sigh into one of the plastic chairs and picked up a shabby magazine. Ramona tried to amuse herself by drawing pictures with her toe in the damp and muddy spots their boots had left on the linoleum.

"Ramona, please don't do that," said Mrs. Quimby, glancing up from her magazine.

Ramona flopped back in a chair and sighed. Her booted feet were beginning to feel hot. To pass the time, she studied pictures of hair styles mounted on the wall. "Is Beezus going to look like *that*?" she whispered.

Mrs. Quimby glanced up again. "I hope not," she whispered back.

Ramona peeked behind the screen and reported to her mother. "A man is washing Beezus's hair, and she's lying back with her head in a sink. He's using gobs of shampoo. He's wasting it."

"Mm-mm." Mrs. Quimby did not raise her

eyes from the magazine. Ramona twisted her head to see what her mother found so interesting. Recipes.

Ramona returned for another look. "He's rubbing her hair with a towel," she reported.

"Mm-mm." Ramona disliked her mother's mm-mming. She walked quietly behind the screen to watch. Lester was studying Beezus's hair, one lock at a time, while a woman, probably a teacher, watched.

"Ramona, come back here," Mrs. Quimby whispered from the edge of the screen.

Once more Ramona flopped down in the plastic chair and swung her legs back and forth. How nice it would be if she could have her hair shampooed, too. She raised her eyebrows as high as she could to make her bangs look longer and thought of her quarter, two nickels, and eight pennies at home in a Q-tip box.

"Little girl, would you like to have your hair

cut?" asked Robert, as if he had read her mind—or was tired of watching her swing her legs.

Ramona stopped swinging her legs and answered politely, "No, thank you. We are scrimping and pinching to make ends meet." Using "scrimping and pinching" made her feel grown-up.

An exasperated sigh escaped Mrs. Quimby. She glanced at her watch. Beezus's haircut was taking longer than she had planned.

"Haircuts for children under ten are half price," said Robert, "and no waiting. We aren't very busy on a wet morning like this."

Mrs. Quimby studied Ramona's hair while Ramona tried to push her eyebrows still higher. "All right, Ramona," she said. "Your hair does need cutting again, and it will help to have one more Saturday chore out of the way."

In a moment Ramona found herself draped

with a poodle-printed plastic sheet and lying back with her hair buried under mounds of lather while a young woman named Denise rubbed her scalp. Such bliss! Washing hair at home was never like this. No soap in her eyes, no having to complain that the water was too hot or too cold, no bumping her head on the kitchen faucet while her knees ached from kneeling on a chair, no one telling her to stop wiggling, no water dribbling down her neck. The shampoo was over much too soon. Denise rubbed Ramona's hair with a towel and guided her to a chair in front of a mirror. On the other side of the row of mirrors, she could hear Beezus's hair being snipped with long pauses between snips.

"She's definitely the pixie type," said the teacher to Denise.

Me? thought Ramona, surprised and pleased.

141

Ramona the pixie sounded much nicer than Ramona the pest as she had so often been called by Beezus and her friends.

"A little off the bangs," said the teacher, "and the ends tapered."

Denise went to work. Her scissors flashed and snipped. Unlike Lester on the other side of the mirror, Denise was sure of what she was doing. Perhaps she had studied longer.

Ramona closed her eyes. *Snip-snip-snip* went her bangs. When she opened her eyes she was surprised to discover they were a tiny bit longer in the center of her forehead. Like the top of a heart, thought Ramona, like a valentine.

Denise lifted locks of wet hair between her fingers and snipped with flying scissors. Lift and snip, all the way around Ramona's head. Flicks of a comb, and Denise aimed a hand-held hair dryer at Ramona's head with one hand while she guided Ramona's hair into place with a brush held in the other. In no time Ramona's hair was dry. More flicks of the comb, the plastic sheet was whisked away, and there sat Ramona with shining hair neatly shaped to her head.

"Excellent," said the teacher to Denise. "She looks adorable."

Students who had no customers gathered around. Ramona could not believe the words she was hearing. "Darling." "Cute as a bug." "A real little pixie." The dryer was humming on the other side of the mirror.

Ramona felt light and happy when she returned to her mother.

"Why, Ramona!" said Mrs. Quimby, laying aside her magazine. "Your hair looks lovely. So neat and shiny."

Ramona couldn't stop smiling, she was so happy. She twitched her nose with joy.

But something made the smile on Mrs. Quimby's face fade. Ramona turned and stared at Beezus standing beside the screen. Her sister's hair had been teased and sprayed until it stood up three inches above her face. Her bangs were plastered in a curve across her forehead.

144

Beezus did not look like an ice skater on television. She looked like an unhappy seventh-grade girl with forty-year-old hair.

Ramona did not know what to say. No one knew what to say except Robert. "You look lovely, dear," he said, but no one answered. Beezus's face looked stiff as her hair.

Ramona thought of the allowance Beezus had saved and wanted to shout at Robert, "She does not look lovely! My sister looks terrible!" For once she kept still. She felt sorry for her sister and sad about the allowance she had saved for so long, but deep inside, where she was ashamed of her feeling, she felt a tiny triumph. Ramona looked nicer than Beezus.

Ramona walked carefully to the car, not wanting to disturb her hair by running and hopping. Beezus walked in stony silence. When all three had buckled their seat belts, Beezus could no longer hold back her feelings. "Well, go ahead and say it!" she burst out in anger and in tears. "Tell me my hair looks terrible. Tell me my hair looks stiff and horrible, like a wig. A *cheap* wig!"

"Now Beezus." Mrs. Quimby spoke gently.

"Well, it *does!* You know it does," Beezus went on. "I tried to tell the man I didn't want my hair to stand up, but he said I would be pleased when he finished, and now I've wasted your whole morning and all my allowance. I look terrible and can't go to school because everyone will laugh at me." She began to sob.

"Dear girl—" Mrs. Quimby took Beezus in her arms and let her weep against her shoulder.

Tears came into Ramona's eyes. She felt she could not bear her sister's unhappiness even if she did look nicer than Beezus. That awful stiff hair, the wasted allowance. . . . Ramona no longer triumphed in looking nicer. She did not want to look nicer. She wanted them to look the same so people would say, There goes that nice-looking Beatrice Quimby and her nice-looking little sister.

"I j-just wanted to look nice." Beezus's voice was muffled by her mother's coat. "I know th-that what I do is more important than how I look, but I just wanted to look nice."

"Of course you do," soothed Mrs. Quimby. "No matter what we say, we all want to look nice."

Ramona sniffed, she felt so sad.

"And you will look nice," Mrs. Quimby continued, "once you wash out all that hair spray and comb your hair. Don't forget Lester cut your hair, and that's what counts."

Beezus raised her soggy tear-stained face. "Do you really think it will look all right when it's washed?"

"Yes, I do," said Mrs. Quimby. "It just needs to be washed and combed."

Beezus sat up and let out an exhausted sigh. Mother and daughter had forgotten their adorable pixie buckled down in the corner of the back seat. Ramona hoped she could make it home without upchucking. She did not want to muss her hair.

6

RAMONA'S NEW PAJAMAS

As Mrs. Quimby had predicted, once Beezus washed her hair she looked like Beezus again. Because they were so glad to see her looking like a seventh-grader, Ramona and her mother did not point out that her new haircut did not look much different from the cuts her mother had given her.

As for Ramona, for a few days grown-ups

said, "Why, how nice your hair looks," as if they were surprised that her hair could look nice.

Children asked, 'How come your bangs are longer in the middle?"

"Because I'm a pixie," Ramona answered, or sometimes, "because I'm a valentine." In a few days everyone forgot about her hair, including Ramona.

Clearly Ramona's parents had something more important on their minds. At first Ramona did not know what it was. She heard long, serious conversations coming from their bedroom, and when she knelt by the furnace outlet to try to catch what they were saying, she could make out only a few words. "I don't . . . school . . . why don't . . . we could . . . teacher . . . school." They sounded as if they might be arguing.

"I told you not to fight anymore!" Ramona yelled through the furnace pipes. There was a startled silence, then laughter from the bedroom. Afterward Ramona could hear only whispers.

Ramona decided her parents must be talking about her. What could they say about Beezus and school? Nothing. What could they say about Ramona and school? To begin with, there was her spelling. . . .

For a while Ramona expected her parents to have one of those little talks with her about really working at her spelling or being a better girl. When they did not, she put their conversations out of her mind and went back to twitching her nose, pretending she was her mother's little rabbit, warm and snug and loved like little bears and bunnies in the books her mother read to her at bedtime when she was little.

One evening, when Ramona had turned from a pixie into a rabbit, she held her feet close together and, twitching her nose, went hopping down the hall. *Thud. Thud. Thud.*

"Ramona, do you have to do that?" asked her mother, who was watching the evening news on television while she let down a hem on a dress for Beezus.

Ramona stopped being her mother's little rabbit, but she did not answer. Of course she did not have to hop. She wanted to. Her mother should know that.

Mrs. Quimby glanced up from her sewing. "Why, Ramona," she remarked, "those pajamas are way too small for you."

And so they were. Ramona, who had been outgrowing clothes all her life, discovered that the sleeves reached only halfway to her wrists, the legs halfway to her ankles, and the seat was too tight. Her pajamas had been washed so often that the fuzz had worn off the flannel.

"I have another pair put away for you," said Mrs. Quimby. "I'll get them and you can change."

"Did Beezus outgrow them?" Ramona was all too familiar with her mother's habit of putting away for Ramona the clothes that Beezus had outgrown several years before.

Mrs. Quimby went to the linen closet. "Not this time. I bought them on sale." She handed Ramona a pair of white pajamas printed with colored balloons. They were so new they were still folded and pinned together.

Ramona quickly pulled out the pins and changed from too-small pajamas into too-big pajamas. The sleeves covered her hands, the legs rumpled around her ankles, and the seat bagged, but oh, how soft and warm and cozy they felt, like the fur of a baby rabbit.

"Just fold up the bottoms so you won't trip," said Mrs. Quimby. "They'll shrink when they're

washed, and you'll grow into them before you know it."

Ramona did as she was told and discovered that, now that her pajamas were no longer tight, she could stoop lower and jump higher. Twitching her nose, she became a rabbit once more and *thump, thump, thumped* down the hall to bed, where she snuggled down, warm and cozy as a little rabbit in a nest, in the pajamas that had never been worn by her sister.

The next morning she awoke still feeling warm and cozy. She lay in bed, not wanting to take off the pajamas, they felt so good.

"Ramona, come along and eat your oatmeal while it's still hot," her mother called to her.

Reluctantly Ramona got out of bed, dabbed a damp washcloth in the middle of her face, and, still in her pajamas, went to breakfast.

"Why, Ramona, you aren't even dressed." Mrs. Quimby, having finished her breakfast, was rinsing her dishes. Mr. Quimby and Beezus were carrying theirs to the sink.

"Don't worry, Mother," said Ramona. "I'm not going to school in my pajamas." As soon as she had spoken Ramona thought how pleasant it would be if she could go to school in her pajamas and feel the soft fuzz against her skin all day.

"Don't dawdle." Mr. Quimby kissed the top of Ramona's head and left for work. Ramona twitched her nose.

Ramona quickly ate her oatmeal—this was easy because oatmeal did not require much chewing—and as she ate she thought about wearing her pajamas to school. Suddenly she recalled seeing the kindergarten class in their red plastic fire hats trooping back from a visit to the fire station, which made her think of her own visit to the firehouse when she was in kindergarten and how she had loved her fire hat. For days afterward, whenever she found even two newspapers piled together, she had called her parents' attention to a fire hazard. She also recalled how astonished she had been to learn that firemen slept in their underwear so that they could jump out of bed and into their clothes if they were called out in the night. Of course, Ramona did not sleep in her underwear, but if she put her clothes on over her pajamas she could pretend to be a fireman anyway.

As Ramona rinsed her dishes she stopped being a rabbit and became a fireman. She raced down the hall and pulled her slacks on over her pajama bottoms. Fortunately, she was not really on her way to fight a fire because she had a hard time stuffing the folded-up legs into her slacks. Then she jerked on her turtleneck sweater over the pajama top. The knitted neck and wristbands hid the flannel nicely. Ramona felt stuffed, but cozy and warm. She remembered to brush her teeth and was ready for school. Like a fireman she pulled on her boots, grabbed her raincoat and hat, and raced into the kitchen for her lunch box.

"By, Mother," she called out as she ran out the back door.

"Where's the fire?" her mother called after her.

How did she guess? Ramona wondered as she ran toward school. Then she decided her mother had not really guessed because she often asked where the fire was when Ramona was in a hurry.

A warm, misty spring rain was falling. Bits of green tipped the black branches of trees. Ramona slowed down to investigate crocus buds like tiny yellow and blue Easter eggs that were pushing up through a neighbor's lawn. Then she ran on as fast as she could in her stuffed

condition, her mouth open, wailing like a fire engine, her boots clomping on the sidewalk. She paid no attention to the people walking to the bus stop who looked at her in surprise. Firemen must get awfully hot, thought Ramona, when she arrived panting and sweating at Glenwood School.

Ramona was glad to sit down on the floor of the cloakroom and pull off her boots. At least her feet felt cooler. She flopped down at her desk. Her face was flushed, and her pajamas no longer felt as soft as a baby rabbit. They were damp with sweat. Maybe pretending to be a fireman wasn't such a good idea after all, thought Ramona, and wondered if anyone would think she looked different. As it turned out, only Davy noticed because Davy always kept an eye on Ramona, who had been chasing him ever since kindergarten. "You look fat," he said.

"I ate a big breakfast," answered Ramona. Then she added, "Davy-in-the-gravy" to keep Davy quiet. She knew he did not like to be called Davy-in-the-gravy.

The classroom seemed unbearably hot, and her clothes felt as tight as the skin on a sausage. As Ramona stood for the flag salute, she wished she had something to unbutton. Later, as she bent over her workbook, she could not help trying to squirm inside her damp clothes.

Mrs. Rudge walked slowly up and down between the desks, looking over shoulders at workbooks. Ramona, finding it difficult to think about her work when she was so uncomfortable, noticed that Davy crooked his arm around his page and bent his head low to hide his work while Becky sat up straight so Mrs. Rudge would be sure to see how perfect her work was. "I like the way Davy keeps his eyes on his own work," said Mrs. Rudge. Davy's ears turned pink with pleasure.

Ramona quickly lowered her eyes to her workbook and remembered that her parents had had more serious talks in their bedroom about school. What was wrong? she wondered again. Mrs. Rudge paused beside her desk to look, not at Ramona's workbook, but at Ramona whose pajamas felt so damp she thought they might be shrinking.

"Ramona, how do you feel this morning?" whispered Mrs. Rudge.

"Fine," answered Ramona, trying to sound as if she spoke the truth.

"Your cheeks are very pink," said Mrs. Rudge. "I think you had better go to the office and ask Mrs. Miller to take your temperature."

"Now?" asked Ramona.

"Yes," said Mrs. Rudge. "Run along."

Ramona laid down her pencil and tried to look thin as she walked out of the room to a rustle of whispers from the class. What was the matter with Ramona? Was she sick? Would she have to be sent home?

Once in the hall she grasped her sweater and pajama top and pulled them up an instant to feel the relief of cool air against her sweaty skin. Then she took hold of both her elastic waistbands and pulled them out and in several times to fan a little cool air inside her slacks.

In the office Mrs. Miller, the school secretary, had Ramona sit on a chair and poked a thermometer under her tongue. "Be sure to keep your lips closed," she said. "We don't want any thermometers falling on the floor and breaking."

Ramona sat still while Mrs. Miller answered the telephone and carried on a long conversation with a mother who was worried about her

164

child's schoolwork and was anxious to talk to the principal. She sat still while a sixth-grade boy came in to use the telephone to call his mother to tell her he had forgotten his lunch money. She sat still while a mother came in to deliver a lunch to a fourth grader who had gone off without it.

Ramona sat and sat. She thought of the long day ahead, of recess and of lunchtime, and began to wish she really were sick. Maybe she was. Maybe she had a fever, a fever so high Mrs. Miller would telephone her mother at work, and her mother would come and take her home and put her to bed between cool white sheets. They would be alone in the house, just the two of them. Her mother would lay her hand on Ramona's hot forehead and give her little treats —ice cream between meals and cold orange juice, not fresh-frozen orange juice but fresh-

fresh orange juice squeezed out of real oranges and not dumped out of a can and thinned with water. Her mother would read aloud stories from library books and would find in the bookcase the books Ramona had loved so much when she was little, especially the one about

the little bear whose mother looked so soft and kind and loving in her long white apron and the book about the bunny snug in bed who said good-night to everything, mittens, a mouse, the moon, and the stars. Later, when Ramona was feeling better, her mother would tuck her upon the couch in the living room so she could watch television and even get to see the ends of old movies.

Pursing her lips tight around the thermometer, Ramona sighed through her nose. Mrs. Miller, her back turned, was busy with the ditto machine.

Finally, when Ramona could not sit still another second, she made a sort of angry humming noise. "M-m-m! M-m-m!"

"Oh, my goodness, Ramona," said Mrs. Miller. "You were so quiet I forgot all about you. Thank you for buzzing like a little bee to remind me." She pulled the thermometer from

167

Ramona's mouth, turned it until she found the silver line that told the temperature, and then said, "Run along back to your room, and tell Mrs. Rudge you're just fine. OK?"

"OK." Ramona was disappointed. Now there would be no rescuing telephone call to her mother, only a long, sweaty day. Oh, well, she knew she would not really have been rescued by her mother, who could not leave her work. Howie's grandmother, accompanied by Willa Jean and probably Woger, would have come for her.

Ramona paused at the drinking fountain for a long, cool drink of water and fanned more air under her clothes before she returned to Room 2.

"What did Mrs. Miller say?" asked Mrs. Rudge.

"She says I'm fine," said Ramona.

Minutes dragged. The seconds between each click of the electric clock seemed to stretch longer and longer. Ramona felt so sleepy she wanted to put her head down on her arms and take a nap.

When the recess bell finally rang, Mrs. Rudge said, "Ramona, would you please come here a minute?"

Reluctantly Ramona walked to Mrs. Rudge's desk.

"Is there something you would like to tell me?" asked the teacher.

Ramona looked up into Mrs. Rudge's brown eyes, then down at the floor, shook her head, and looked up at Mrs. Rudge once more. Her teacher seemed so kind, so soft and plump, that Ramona longed to lean against her and tell her all her troubles, how hot she was and how no one ever said she was her mother's girl and how

169

she wanted her mother to love her like a little rabbit and how somehow all these feelings had led to pretending to be a fireman.

"I can keep a secret," said Mrs. Rudge. "I promise."

This encouragement was all Ramona needed. "I—I'm too warm," she confessed. "I've got my pajamas on." Please, please, Mrs. Rudge, don't make me tell why, she prayed, because now that she had confessed she felt that wearing pajamas to school was a silly thing to do. A second-grader pretending to be a fireman—it was the dumbest thing she had ever imagined.

"Why, that's no problem," said Mrs. Rudge. "Just go to the girls' bathroom and take off your pajamas." She reached into a drawer and pulled out a paper bag. "Roll up your pajamas and put them in this bag and hide them in your desk."

Ramona shook her head. "I can't." As soon as she had spoken, she realized she had chosen the wrong words. Now Mrs. Rudge would say, There's no such word as *can't,* and Ramona would argue with herself all over again. How could there not be such a word as *can't*? Mrs. Rudge had just said *can't* so *can't* had to be a word.

To Ramona's relief, Mrs. Rudge merely said, "Why not?"

"I don't have any underwear on," confessed Ramona. Was there amusement in Mrs. Rudge's warm brown eyes? There better not be. No, it was all right. Mrs. Rudge was not laughing at her.

"I see," said the teacher. "That *is* a problem, but I don't think you need to worry about it. Your slacks and sweater are warm enough on a day like this."

"You mean go without any underwear?" Ramona was a little shocked at the suggestion. In summer she did not wear an undershirt, but she had always worn underpants, even in the hottest weather.

"Why not?" asked Mrs. Rudge with a wave of her hand, as if she were waving away underwear as unimportant. Underwear—pooh!

"Well . . ." said Ramona, halfway agreeing. "But . . . promise you won't tell my mother what I did?"

"I promise," said Mrs. Rudge with a big smile. "Now run along before you melt into a puddle right here on the floor."

Ramona did as she was told, and, oh, the relief she felt in the girls' bathroom when she shut herself in a cubicle and peeled off those damp pajamas, which, to her surprise, had not shrunk at all. She quickly pulled on her clothes and rolled up the pajamas as tight as she could and hid them in the paper bag. Even though skipping in the halls was forbidden, Ramona skipped. The halls were empty, recess was over, and she was late, but still she skipped because she felt as light and as cool as a spring breeze. And who would know she was not wearing underwear? Nobody, that's who. Maybe wearing underwear wasn't so important after all. Maybe after today Ramona would skip underwear—at least in summer when she was wearing slacks.

Back in Room 2, Ramona lifted the lid of her desk and hid her package way at the back

behind her books. She pretended not to notice the curious stares of the boys and girls, who were wondering why Mrs. Rudge said nothing about Ramona's being late. Instead she looked at Mrs. Rudge, who gave her a tiny smile that said quite plainly, We have a secret, just the two of us.

Ramona's heart was warm with love for her teacher. She smiled back and twitched her nose like a bunny.

7

THE TELEPHONE CALL

By the time school was over Ramona had forgotten about the pajamas in her desk, and that evening she was so busy practicing her name in cursive writing that they remained forgotten. No more babyish printing for Ramona. Mrs. Rudge had taught her to write in what Ramona used to call "that rumply stuff." And write she did.

Ramona Quimby

She wrote in pencil, ballpoint pen, and crayon on any paper she could find—paper bags, old envelopes, the backs of arithmetic papers, around the edge of the newspaper. She wrote her name with her finger in steam on the bathroom mirror when her father had taken a shower after work. Before supper she wrote her name in dust on the top of the television set. After supper she went outside where, beneath the porch light, she wrote Ramona Quimby in chalk on each of the front steps. When she came back into the house, she found her mother and Beezus on the couch studying pictures in a paperback book.

"Let me see, too," said Ramona, wiping her chalky fingers on the seat of her slacks and twitching her nose.

"It's just a book on how to cut hair that I ran across," said Mrs. Quimby. "I thought I would try to learn to cut Beezus's hair so it would look like the ice skater on television."

"See, Mother," said Beezus. "First you twist the top hair up out of the way and cut the bottom hair first."

"I see," said Mrs. Quimby. "That doesn't look so difficult."

Ramona felt left out. Somehow that trip to the beauty school had brought her mother and Beezus closer together. They were friends again, close friends.

"Bedtime, Ramona," said Mrs. Quimby, still studying the book.

A terrible thought crossed Ramona's mind. Her new pajamas! She had left them rolled up in her desk at school. Then Ramona had an even worse thought. This was Friday. She could not bring her pajamas home until Monday. How could she explain if her family found out?

Ramona made up her mind right then and there that neither her parents nor Beezus would find out because she was going to keep those pajamas a secret. Without waiting for a second reminder Ramona was in and out of the bathtub in no time. She could not locate the old pajamas she had taken off the night before, but she did come across another too-small pair in a drawer. She put them on, turned off the light, hopped into bed, and pulled the covers up tight around her ears. But what if she fell asleep before her parents came in to kiss her goodnight?

Ramona took no chances. "Come and kiss me good-night," she sang out while hanging on tight to the sheet and blankets.

Mr. Quimby was first. "What's got into you,

Ramona?" he asked after he had kissed her. "You forgot to beg to stay up just a little longer to watch TV or finish drawing a picture or read another chapter. You forgot to remind us you don't have to go to school tomorrow. Don't you feel good?"

Ramona giggled. "Daddy, you're so silly. I feel fine." She was pleased that her father had noticed she now read books with chapters.

Mrs. Quimby was next. Ramona pulled the covers tight around her ears when she heard her mother coming down the hall. Mrs. Quimby kissed Ramona and then looked at her in the dim light from the hall. "Are you cold?" she asked.

"No," answered Ramona.

"If you are, I can get another blanket from the linen closet," said Mrs. Quimby. Then she added, "Nighty-night. Sweet dreams."

That was close, thought Ramona with a twitch

of her nose. When she said her prayers, she added a request at the end. Please, God, do not let anyone find out I wore my pajamas to school. She felt that although God was probably too busy to think about her pajamas, asking would not hurt and might even help.

Saturday morning she dressed in the closet and hid the too-small pajamas in her bottom drawer. She was happy to discover that her father was home for the morning, even though he would have to work at the Shop-Rite Market Saturday afternoon and evening. Today was going to be a good day. The sun was shining, the sidewalk dry, and her father could watch her skate.

That is, she was happy until Mr. Quimby looked around the living room and said, "This is a home, not a base camp." He had recently watched a television program on mountain climbing. "Let's all pitch in and clean this place up. Ramona, pick up all the newspapers and magazines and dust the living room. Beezus, you can run the vacuum cleaner. Then both of you tackle your rooms. Change the sheets and straighten up. Every kettle must rest on its own bottom around here." He did not mention that this was one of his grandmother's sayings.

Except for washing the egg beater in sudsy water so she could beat up a lot of suds, Ramona did not care much for housework, and this morning she longed to be outside racing up and down the sidewalk on her roller skates. However, she carried the old newspapers out to the garage without complaining and hastily flicked a dustcloth around the living room while Beezus plugged in the vacuum cleaner and made it growl back and forth across the carpet. Mr. Quimby went off to clean the bathroom while Mrs. Quimby was busy in the kitchen.

In a playful mood Beezus pushed the vacuum

cleaner right up to Ramona's shoes. Ramona squealed as if she expected the vacuum cleaner to nibble her toes. Beezus pursued her with the vacuum cleaner. Around the carpet they went until Ramona said, "Ha-ha, you can't catch me!" and crawled behind the couch. Beezus returned to running the vacuum cleaner properly, back and forth in straight lines, the way their father mowed the lawn.

Ramona sat hugging her knees behind the couch. She was in no hurry, as her father put it, to tackle her room.

Ramona sat there behind the couch, a kettle resting on its bottom, thinking. She thought how embarrassed she would be if her family found out she had worn her pajamas to school. She thought about her mother and Beezus and what good friends they had become, almost as if they were the same age.

As Ramona sat letting these thoughts slide

through her mind, the telephone rang in the kitchen. Above the growl of the vacuum cleaner, she heard her mother say, "Why he*llo*!" as if she were surprised to hear from the person calling.

Who had surprised her mother? Ramona listened hard. Beezus must have been curious, too, for she turned off the vacuum cleaner, which made eavesdropping easier for Ramona.

"Oh . . . ? Yes . . . Yes . . . Oh, does she?" Mrs. Quimby went on in a friendly polite voice quite different from the friendly voice she used when she talked to her sister, the girls' Aunt Beatrice.

Who does what? Ramona wondered, alert, since she was usually the one who had done something. Her mother laughed. Ramona felt indignant without knowing why. She could not think of anything she had done that anyone would telephone her mother about.

Mrs. Quimby continued for some time, but

Ramona could make no sense out of the conversation. Finally her mother said, "Thank you for telling me, Mrs. Rudge." Then she hung up.

The sound of her teacher's name gave Ramona a strange feeling, as if she were in an elevator that had suddenly gone down when she expected it to go up. When she stopped feeling as if the floor had dropped beneath her, she was furious. So that was why her mother had laughed. Mrs. Rudge had told! She had telephoned her mother and tattled. And her mother thought it was funny! Ramona would never forgive either of them. Never, never, *never.*

Beezus turned on the vacuum cleaner again. Ramona crawled on her hands and knees from behind the couch and was surprised to see that her mother had come into the living room. "What have you been doing back there?" asked Mrs. Quimby.

"Resting on my bottom," said Ramona with a scowl.

Beezus switched off the vacuum cleaner again. Her turn had come to foresee an interesting argument.

Ramona faced her mother. "Mrs. Rudge told!" she shouted. "And she promised she would never tell. And then you had to go and laugh!"

"Now calm down." Mrs. Quimby plucked a fluff of dust from Ramona's sleeve.

"I *won't* calm down!" yelled Ramona so loud her father came down the hall to see what was going on. "I *hate* Mrs. Rudge! She's a tattletale. She doesn't love me and she tells fibs!" Ramona saw her mother and father exchange a familiar look that said, Which of us is going to handle this one?

"*Hate* is a strong word, Ramona," said Mrs. Quimby quietly.

"Not strong enough," said Ramona.

186

"This looks like nine on the Richter scale," said Mr. Quimby, as if Ramona were an earthquake.

"And you and Daddy talk about me in your room at night," Ramona stormed at her mother.

"Someday, Ramona," said her father, "you are going to have to learn that the world does not revolve around you."

"I don't care what Mrs. Rudge says," shouted Ramona. "I didn't leave my pajamas at school on purpose. I forgot."

Mrs. Quimby looked astonished. "Left your pajamas— What on earth are your pajamas doing at school?" She was plainly trying to stifle a laugh.

Ramona was both surprised and bewildered. If her mother did not know about her pajamas, what could Mrs. Rudge have said?

"What on earth are your pajamas doing at school?" Ramona's mother asked again.

The whole story—her feeling that the flannel was as soft as bunny fur and how she pretended to be a fireman so she wouldn't have to take her pajamas off—flashed through Ramona's mind and embarrassed her. "I won't tell," she said, folding her arms defiantly.

"She probably took them for Show and Tell," volunteered Beezus.

Ramona gave her sister a look of contempt. Second graders in Mrs. Rudge's room did not have Show and Tell every day, only when someone had something really important and educational to bring such as a butterfly that had hatched out of a cocoon in a jar. And Beezus should know that no second grader would take pajamas to school for Show and Tell. That would be too babyish even for kindergarten. Beezus knew these things. She had been through them all. She was just trying to make Ramona look babyish.

Ramona was about to shout, I did not! but decided this would be unwise. Beezus had supplied a reason, a very weak reason, why she might have taken her pajamas to school.

Apparently Mrs. Quimby did not accept Beezus's explanation either, for she said, "Your pajamas did not get out of bed and run along beside you to school. Oh, well, I don't suppose it matters."

Ramona scowled. Her mother need not think she could win her over by being funny. She was mad and she was going to stay mad. She was mad at Beezus for always being her mother's girl. She was mad at her teacher for telling her mother something (*what*?) She was mad at her parents for not being upset because she was mad. She was mad at herself for letting it out that she had left her pajamas at school.

"Nobody likes me. Nobody in the whole world," said Ramona, warming to her subject as the cat walked disdainfully through the room on his way to peace on Beezus's bed. "Not even my own mother and father. Not even the cat. Beezus gets all the attention around here. Even Picky-picky likes Beezus more than he likes me!" She was pleased that her father stayed in the living room and she didn't lose any of her audience. "You'll be sorry someday when I'm rich and famous."

"I didn't know you were planning to be rich and famous," said Mr. Quimby.

Neither had Ramona until that moment.

"What do you mean, I get all the attention around here?" demanded Beezus. "Nobody tapes my schoolwork to the refrigerator door. We can hardly find the refrigerator, it is so buried under all your drawings and junk!"

Both parents looked at Beezus in surprise. "Why, Beezus," said Mrs. Quimby, "I had no idea you minded."

"Well, I do," said Beezus crossly. "And Ramona always gets out of things like washing dishes because she is too little. She'll probably still be too little when she's eighty."

"See?" said Ramona. "Beezus doesn't like me because my artwork is stuck to the refrigerator." Her parents weren't supposed to feel sorry for Beezus. They were supposed to feel sorry for Ramona.

"I'm always in the way," said Ramona. "You have to park me with Howie's grandmother so you can go to work, and Howie's grandmother doesn't like me. She thinks I'm so terrible she probably won't want me around anymore, and then there won't be anybody to look after me and you can't go to work. So there!" Ramona flopped down on the couch, waiting for someone to tell her she was wrong.

Ramona's mother and father said nothing.

"Everybody picks on me all the time," said

Ramona. Maybe she really would be so bad Mrs. Kemp would say, I simply cannot put up with Ramona another day.

Silence.

Ramona made up her mind to shock her parents, really shock them. "I am going to run away," she announced.

"I'm sorry to hear that," said Mr. Quimby as if running away were a perfectly natural thing to do.

"When are you leaving?" inquired Ramona's mother politely. The question was almost more than Ramona could bear. Her mother was supposed to say, Oh, Ramona, please, please don't leave me!

"Today," Ramona managed to say with quivering lips. "This morning."

"She just wants you to feel sorry for her," said heartless Beezus. "She wants you to stop her."

Ramona waited for her mother or father to say something, but neither spoke. Finally there was nothing for Ramona to do but get up from the couch. "I guess I'll go pack," she said, and started slowly toward her room.

No one tried to prevent her. When she reached her room, tears began to fall. She got out her Q-tip box with all her money, forty-three cents, in it. Still no one came to beg her not to leave. She looked around for something in which to pack, but all she could find was an old doll's nursing kit. Ramona unzipped it and placed her Q-tip box inside. She added her best box of crayons and a pair of clean socks. Outside she heard the cheerful *ching-chong, ching-chong* of roller skates on cement. Some children were happy.

If nobody stopped her, where would she run to? Not Howie's house, even though Howie was no longer mad at her. His grandmother was

not paid to look after her on Saturday. She could take the bus to Aunt Beatrice's apartment house, but Aunt Beatrice would bring her back home. Maybe she could live in the park and sleep under the bushes in the cold. Poor little Ramona, all alone in the park, shivering in the dark. Well, at least it was not raining. That was something. And there were no big wild animals, just chipmunks.

She heard her mother coming down the hall. Tears stopped. Ramona was about to be rescued. Now her mother would say, Please don't run away. We love you and want you to stay.

Instead Mrs. Quimby walked into the bedroom with a suitcase in one hand and two bananas in the other. "You will need something to pack in," she told Ramona. "Let me help." She opened the suitcase on the unmade bed and placed the bananas inside. "In case you get hungry," she explained.

Ramona was too shocked to say anything. Mothers weren't supposed to help their children run away. "You'll need your roller skates in case you want to travel fast," said Mrs. Quimby. "Where are they?"

As if she were walking in her sleep, Ramona pulled her roller skates from a jumble of toys in the bottom of her closet and handed them to her mother, who placed them at the bottom of the suitcase. How could her mother not love a little girl like Ramona?

"Always pack heavy things at the bottom," advised Mrs. Quimby. "Now where are your boots in case it rains?" She looked around the room. "And don't forget your Betsy book. And your little box of baby teeth. You wouldn't want to leave your teeth behind."

Ramona felt she could run away without her old baby teeth, and she was hurt that her mother did not want to keep them to remember her by.

She stood watching while her mother packed briskly and efficiently.

"You will want Ella Funt in case you get lonely," said Mrs. Quimby.

When Ramona said her mother did not love her, she had no idea her mother would do a terrible thing like this. And her father. Didn't he care either? Apparently not. He was too busy scrubbing the bathroom to care that Ramona was in despair. And what about Beezus? She was probably secretly glad Ramona was going to run away because she could have her parents all to herself. Even Picky-picky would be glad to see the last of her.

As Ramona watched her mother fold underwear for her to take away, she began to understand that deep down inside in the place where her secret thoughts were hidden, she had never really doubted her mother's love for her. Not until now. . . . She thought of all the things her mother had done for her, the way she had sat up most of the night when Ramona had an earache, the birthday cake she had made in the shape of a cowboy boot all frosted with chocolate with lines of white icing that looked like stitching. That was the year she was four and had wanted cowboy boots more than anything, and her parents had given her real ones as well. She thought of the way her mother reminded her to brush her teeth. Her mother would not do that unless she cared about her teeth, would she? She thought of the time her mother let her get her hair cut at the beauty school, even though they had to scrimp and pinch. She thought of the gentle books about bears and bunnies her mother had read at bedtime when she was little.

"There." Mrs. Quimby closed the suitcase,

snapped the latches, and set it on the floor. "Now you are all packed." She sat down on the bed.

Ramona pulled her car coat out of the closet and slowly put it on, one arm and then the other. She looked at her mother with sad eyes as she grasped the handle of her suitcase and lifted. The suitcase would not budge. Ramona grasped it with both hands. Still she could not lift it.

Hope flowed into Ramona's heart. Had her mother made the suitcase too heavy on purpose? She looked closely at her mother, who was watching her. She saw—didn't she?—a tiny smile in her mother's eyes.

"You tricked me!" cried Ramona. "You made the suitcase too heavy on purpose. You don't want me to run away!"

"I couldn't get along without my Ramona," said Ramona's mother. She held out her arms.

Ramona ran into them. Her mother had said the words she had longed to hear. Her mother could not get along without her. She felt warm and safe and comforted and oh, how good her mother smelled, so clean and sweet like flowers. Better than any mother in the whole world. Ramona's tears dampened her mother's blouse. After a moment Mrs. Quimby handed Ramona a Kleenex. When Ramona had wiped her eyes and nose, she was surprised to discover that her mother had tears in her eyes, too.

"Mama," said Ramona, using a word she had given up as babyish, "why did you do that?"

"Because I could see I couldn't get anyplace arguing with you," answered her mother. "You wouldn't listen."

The truth made Ramona uncomfortable. "Why did Mrs. Rudge phone?" she asked, to change the subject.

Mrs. Quimby looked concerned. "She called

to say that she had noticed you twitching your nose a lot—Daddy and I have noticed it, too—and she wondered if something was making you nervous. She wondered if you perhaps needed a shorter day in school."

And a longer day with Howie's grandmother? What a terrible idea. "School is easy," said Ramona, not mentioning spelling, which, after all, might be easy if she paid more attention to it.

"Have you any idea what makes you twitch your nose?" asked Mrs. Quimby gently. "I noticed you twitch it three times during breakfast."

Ramona was surprised. Maybe she had twitched so much she could twitch without knowing it. "Of course I know why," she said. "I was pretending I was a rabbit, a baby rabbit, because you call me a little rabbit sometimes."

This time Ramona did not mind when her mother laughed. She laughed a bit, too, to show that she now thought pretending to be a baby rabbit seemed silly, as if it were something she had done a long time ago when she was little.

"Rabbits are nice," said Mrs. Quimby, "but I prefer a little girl. My little girl."

"Really?" said Ramona, even though she knew her mother spoke the truth.

"I am glad to know you were a little rabbit," said Ramona's mother. "I was afraid my working full time might be too much for you, and just when we have decided Daddy will quit his job at the market and go back to school."

Ramona was astonished. "School! You mean do homework and stuff like that? Daddy?"

"I expect so," answered Mrs. Quimby.

"Why does he want to go and do a thing like that?" Ramona could not understand.

"To finish college," her mother explained. "So he can get a better job, he hopes. One that he likes."

So this was what her parents had been talking about at night in their room. "Will he have to go away?" asked Ramona.

"No. He can go to Portland State right here in town," explained Mrs. Quimby. "But I will have to go on working full time, which I want to do anyway because I like my job. Do you think you can manage to get along with Mrs. Kemp?"

Ramona thought how much happier her family would be if her father never came home tired from working in the express line again. "Of course I can," she agreed with courage. "I've gotten along—sort of—so far." After this she would stay away from pinking shears and bluing. As for Willa Jean—maybe she would go to nursery school and learn to shape up. Yes, Ramona could manage. "And I guess we'll have to scrimp and pinch some more," she said.

"That's right. Scrimp and pinch and save as much money as we can while Daddy is studying, even though he hopes to find part-time work after school starts," said Mrs. Quimby. "And by the way, you don't have to tell me if you don't want to, but I am curious. Why are your pajamas at school?"

"Oh." Ramona made a face; it all seemed so ridiculous now. She gave her mother the shortest possible explanation.

Mrs. Quimby did not seem upset. She merely said, "What next?" and laughed.

"Did Mrs. Rudge say anything about my spelling?" Ramona hesitated to ask the question, but she did want to know the answer.

"Why, no," said Mrs. Quimby. "She didn't even mention spelling, but she did say you were one of her little sparklers who made teaching interesting." And with that Ramona's mother left the room.

A little sparkler! Ramona liked that. She thought of the last Fourth of July when she had twirled through the dusk, a sparkler fizzing and spitting in each hand and leaving circles of light and figure eights as she had spun across the front yard until she had fallen to the grass with dizziness. And now she was one of Mrs. Rudge's little sparklers!

Ramona held out her arms and twirled across the room, pretending she was holding sparklers. Then she seized a pencil and paper that were lying on her bureau and wrote her name in good, bold cursive:

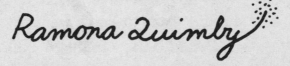

There. A girl who was a sparkler needed a

name that looked like a sparkler. And that was the way Ramona Quimby was going to write her name.

Ching-chong, ching-chong went the roller skates out on the sidewalk. Ramona opened the suitcase and pulled out her skates.